Other Ways of Being

Other Ways of Being

Gill James

Bridge House

British Library Cataloguing in Publication Data
A Record of this Publication is available from the British
Library

ISBN 978-1-907335-67-9

This edition published 2019 by Bridge House Publishing
Manchester, England

Contents

Dancing to the Moon

The first time I set eyes on Patrick O'Leary what I had left of a heart almost jumped out of my chest. All I could see to start with were his soft blond curls I wanted to touch and his smiling blue eyes I wanted to have looking into mine forever. Then I saw him dance and I knew that I wanted to be his only dancing partner. For eternity.

I shouldn't have even been there. I'm only sixteen. They're very strict at the Clerkenwell Arms, especially when the Irish dance trials are on. But it was a new moon that night so I guess I was at my best. Talbot had warned me that I would still have a monthly cycle of sorts though it would be very different from before. And spot on, it follows the moon. This is always my shining day, the day of the new moon.

I've been like this for over a year now and I'm getting used to it. I can never remember the details of the moonless nights, but the next day I'm always full of energy, and confident and look much older and very glamorous. So, what with the lipstick, and the short skirt and that bitchy glow inside, I got in without them even asking for ID. I even bought a glass of wine for form's sake. No sweat.

It was the music that made me go in. The music and a need for some warmth. Some human warmth that is – I don't notice the winter's cold any more. And I guess it was because I was just in that sort of mood. New moon day. Daredevil day.

I couldn't take my eyes off him as he danced. Back and neck straight. Gaze fixed. Arms rigid by his sides. His feet never missed a beat and always came down in exactly the right place. My own feet started tapping to the music.

I used to dance when I was a little girl. Lots of us do. I never got all that far with it, though I was not at all bad. I

6

just got into other things. Like you do. But I can still remember all of the steps.

He started dancing around the room. He paused at each table where any good-looking female sat. His feet still worked, of course. I had to exercise so much self-control not to go over to those hussies and scratch their eyes out or tear out their hair. He was sweating slightly and his manly, slightly musky smell was getting to me. There were others in the room, other good-looking young men, some of whom were also dancers, but I only had eyes – and a nose – for him.

At last he paused by my table and fixed me with his eyes. Tap, tap, tap, tap, tappity tap, went his feet, as if they were asking a question. A faint smile opened his lips, his eyebrows rose slightly. His pupils grew large. He was taking me in, was he? The bitch inside smirked but I tried to keep my gaze neutral. Tapity tap. Tap, tap. He nodded.

I got up from the table. My feet began to work. Yes, I remembered the steps. It was easy, especially with all this energy. In fact I had to keep it in check a little, or somebody would have noticed something. I didn't even break a sweat or get out of breath. He was breathing hard by now yet he still kept exact time and rhythm. I loved him for that. I loved him because he was finding it tiring now and was still being perfect. The smell of him made my head light.

We were close at times. The place was so full there was barely a dance floor. We almost touched but not quite. As our shoulders and hands came within inches of each other I felt an exchange of energy. Tingles crackled through my body and I had the feeling that he gained some energy from me. We moved lightly around one another, our eyes and our feet in conversation. This was ecstasy. This I wanted forever. Tap, tap, tappity tap.

The music stopped. It had to eventually. It felt as though

7

a thread between us was broken. The crowd in the pub started clapping and cheering. He was a little out of breath.

"Patrick O'Leary," he whispered.

"Fyonah McBride," I whispered back.

He nodded and held up his hand to shush the crowd. "Ladies, and gentlemen," he cried. "Fyonah McBride."

The crowd cheered and hooted.

He turned to me and grinned. "Fyonah McBride," he said, "will you dance with me again?"

I nodded. "Of course," I said. Why wouldn't I? Why wouldn't I dance with this man forever?

He kissed me on the cheek. "Thank you," he said.

Now I was breathless.

But then he was surrounded by all the trial officials, and people who were obviously his friends and fans. The moon was rising. A tiny slither of common sense crept back in. This wouldn't work. I was an underage school girl, with a strange monthly cycle, who had school tomorrow. Better just to go home and dream about him.

The second time I saw Patrick O'Leary I was on the bus two days later coming home from school. He got on at the corner of O'Malley Row and took one look at us all and went back downstairs. He looked straight at me actually, but I thank God that all he seemed to see was just another St Catherine's girl in green. Green's not my colour. Red and purple suit me now. And thank the lord all of us girls in this boring little Irish town decided that we wanted ankle length skirts for our uniform or he might have recognised my legs. But there was still enough time for those clear blue eyes of his to send a shockwave through my body.

I saw him the third time in the village chip shop the next day. I walked straight into him. He was coming in as I was

8

going out. I almost dropped my chips my hands were shaking so much.

"Fyonah McBride," he said. "I'm glad to see you're keeping your strength up. But have you been hiding from me? I need you to dance with me again. So when's it to be then? Hmm?" He lifted my chin up and made me look at him.

I almost forgot to breathe. He was so lovely. Lovelier in real life than he'd been in all the dreams I'd made up about him. That look was what I wanted. That face.

He smiled.

"Go eat your chips," he said. "But come tonight. Half past six. The Arcadia Rooms. Above O Brien's. Don't be late." He touched my cheek and then carried on into the chip shop.

I didn't eat the chips, of course. What would somebody with a body like mine want with fat, greasy chips? As usual, I served them to all the stray cats and dogs I could find between the chippy and our house, preserving just a few as evidence.

"Fyonah, are you going to have your tea?" Daddy called as I went in through the back.

"I've had chips, Daddy, look," I replied, showing him the almost empty packet.

"Well, you know what your mummy said, if you don't start eating properly…"

"Yes, and he'll only say the same as before," I said.

"You're sure those chips were enough?" he went on.

"Sure, Daddy."

Last time, four months ago, I'd refused to see anybody but Talbot when they'd insisted I saw a doctor.

"He's a strange man," said Mummy. "Are you sure you wouldn't rather see that nice new lady doctor."

"Talbot or nobody," I'd replied.

They just put that down in the end to more of my teenage quirkiness.

"She's not eating properly," Mummy had said to the doctor. "She doesn't sit down at the table with us anymore."

That was true. I usually took my food up to my room, disposed of it somehow and then brought the empty plate down later.

"That doesn't matter so much," said Talbot. "As long as she is getting enough nutrition, and she looks bonny enough to me."

He weighed and measured me and mumbled "Fine," several times.

Then he looked meaningfully at me. "And the – er – monthly cycle is going all right? There may be changes... as you grow..."

I nodded.

"You know what Dr Talbot said last time," I said to Daddy and escaped to my room.

I spent the rest of the afternoon working through my wardrobe trying to decide what to wear for Patrick.

Six evenings in a row we danced and hardly spoke. Tap, tap, tappity tap. It was as though our feet did the talking. My energy was holding up. And he was fit – both ways – and strong. We grew to know each other well even though we didn't talk. We communicated through our feet. And every evening he walked me home and kissed me before I went in. Just lightly. That daredevil in me wanted more from him.

"What about your school work?" said Mummy.

"Not a problem," I said. It wasn't. I just did it at night while they slept.

"Fyonah..." warned Daddy.

Butt out!

The seventh evening was the end of the trials.

"The couple we want to go forward," announced the judge, "are Fyonah McBride and Patrick O'Leary."

He hugged me and kissed my hair. "My good girl," he whispered.

As we walked to my home that night he talked more than he had the rest of the time we'd been together. He held my hand and squeezed it tight. We were just like any other couple. When we got to my house, he pulled me into the shadows. And kissed me really hard this time. And though, as we got to the middle of the month, the daredevil was calming a little I still wanted more.

"Oh Fyonah McBride," he said as he pulled away from me, "I think I'm falling in love with you."

Well, good. Then, panic. If there was no dancing tomorrow, would I see him? All day and all night was already too long to be away from him. Could I bear even one evening alone?

"Can I see you tomorrow?" he asked. "Even though there's no dancing?"

We walked through the woods. Odd, he didn't seem to mind the cold. Naturally, I didn't. It was a fine evening otherwise, with the moon one night off full and shining brightly. A romantic dream. But common sense was kicking in fast. I couldn't do this anymore.

I stopped walking and held back. "I'm only sixteen and I'm still at school," I said as quickly as I could.

His face did not move at first. Then his eyes crinkled into a smile and I had the sensation of my heart leaping.

"I know," he said. "I saw you that day on the bus. That's why I've been careful."

"But I am sixteen," I said.

He pulled me back towards him and kissed me properly.

"Fyonah, oh my Fyonah," he whispered, "dance with me forever."

Oh, I would, I would. I ran my fingers through his hair. That musky smell about him was even stronger tonight and

I loved him all the more for it. He pulled me gently to the ground. I could not get enough of him and he seemed just as eager.

Afterwards, as we were walking home, he sighed. He stopped walking and turned to face me.

"Oh, Fyonah," he said, "I cannot see you tomorrow. Just the one time."

"Can't I come with you?" I asked. "Where do you have to be?"

"No, you really can't, my love. You really can't." He touched my cheek and turned my face so that I was looking into those lovely blue eyes. "But the day after, there'll be the dancing again. And after that…"

I had to be content. His eyes told me that he really meant it, that I couldn't go with him. But they also told me that he would be back and that it wasn't just that he'd got what he wanted and was ready to move on. And I loved him all the more for it.

I didn't know what to do with myself the next evening. I was no longer content to dream of my man-boy. I wanted him with me now and always. Despite the full moon which should have brought some sanity and smothered the daredevil, she was still there, hanging on.

I decided to try to run off my frustration and made for the woods where Patrick had loved me the night before. I was trying to relive those sweet moments. The memory was so strong that I could smell him but the lack of him as so great that I could feel tears stinging my eyes though I know I can no longer cry.

Then I saw a flash of green. A man's jumper. Someone in the woods in front of me. That way of walking unmistakable. So it wasn't a memory causing to me to smell him. He was there and his scent was stronger than ever. What did it remind me of? Man? Dog? Fox? Animal-like anyway. His smell but more of it. It made my ghost heart beat so strongly that it became a physical pain. Why was he here in the woods again? Did he have another lover?

If he did and I found her, I'd kill her for sure.

"Your emotions will calm mid-cycle," Talbot had said. "This is the best time to kill for vengeance rather than food. You're calm enough to calculate, to use good judgement, yet still strong enough to kill swiftly and cleanly. Avoid leaving evidence at all costs."

My mid-cycle always coincided with the full moon. So, yes, I would kill but I wasn't calm. Talbot was only half right.

Patrick suddenly dropped to the ground. He howled. If my heart could actually beat it would have stopped now. I realised now why he had to avoid me tonight. He too has a pesky cycle. A moon-determined cycle.

This was dangerous for me, more dangerous than if I were a normal girl but the daredevil and the girl who loves Patrick were both too fascinated to move away. I watched the change.

You know, it isn't how they show it in the movies or tell it in the books. Well, not in Patrick's case anyway. He danced into it. He swirled and turned. Gracefully and lightly. Like when he's at the trials. Like when he's with me. With each turn he became hairier, more animal-like, more wolf than boy.

His clothes and his flesh both turned into fur. Gently. Subtly. His eyes glazed over, lost their humanness. He began to drool, spittle streaking his fur silver. And that wonderful musky smell just got stronger and stronger. It made me want him so much – Patrick, that is, not the wolf. Then he turned and howled at the moon.

When he looked back at me his eyes were all wolf. And then a flash of Patrick. Was he looking at me, his lover, or

13

at his greatest enemy? I should have gone by now but I could still only stare.

"Werewolves are our greatest threat," Talbot told me just after the change. "The best time to fight them is at the middle of the cycle. You can also outrun them then – though why you would try to when you can kill, no one of our kind would know."

Where could I run to? This island is not big enough.

"You can't outswim them," Talbot had said. "If the water's too wide for one stride, jump from boat to boat but don't be seen."

He's was still looking at me, the wolf. He should have jumped by now. Those could not be Patrick's eyes. Talbot said the wolves never remember their human existence until the sun comes up. But he knew something. This wolf did.

I needed to run.

If I was to be Patrick O Leary's dancing partner again I must run and run until the sun came up.

He snarled, then howled and bore his teeth. He nodded his head, almost pointing the way I should go. Still he didn't spring like Talbot told me he would.

"I'll see you tomorrow, my Patrick," I whispered.

I turned and set the daredevil and the energy that's left into running my fastest, over fields, though woods, jumping from hilltop to hilltop and then from boat to boat, ignoring the howls and growls and snapping teeth behind me.

"I will outrun you, Wolf O'Leary," became my mantra. "For tomorrow I need to dance with my lover."

I ran and ran. The first rays of the sun appeared over the horizon. The moon began to sink. But the howls were just as frequent and the musky smell seemed stronger than ever even though he was behind me.

"He should be getting human again by now," I thought. Even my extraordinary energy was going. I could have turned and faced him… But I might have killed my lover or he might have killed me.

I was getting weaker. Was it possible? Could one of my kind die of exhaustion? Never!

A pain shot up my back. How could this be? We are not supposed to feel pain. Something was gripping me and I could no longer hear him behind me. Wolf teeth in my side.

This would not do. I felt the blood charging round my body, preparing me for the attack. The monster in me wanted to tear off the wolf's head.

"Remember he's your Patrick, your lover," the girl in me whispered. I held back for a split second but then felt a snarl rising in my throat. I had his head in my hands now and I bent towards his neck, ready to bite. His musky smell was driving me into a different sort of frenzy this time.

The sun suddenly dazzled me as it slipped finally over the horizon. The moon had gone. A human hand was holding mine.

"Fyonah MacBride, will you dance with me forever now?" said my Patrick as he smiled at me out of his twinkling blue eyes. "Only don't run so fast and so far the next time I try to ask you."

I bit my lip and frowned. I'd almost killed him, my precious Patrick.

He touched me lightly on the cheek.

"Hey Fyonah MacBride," he said softly. "Don't you worry now. We'll get this cycle under control. We'll dance to the moon."

Then I knew that Patrick O'Leary would be my dancing partner for eternity.

Cloning

I wonder whether these are her favourites as well. It's highly likely I guess. I've seen the others do the same: wash the maroon tights out overnight rather than pick another colour for the next day. Why don't we just buy a job lot of maroon ones and be done with it? I daren't suggest it though. She, the real Moira, might accuse me of being up myself. As if.

M27 is irritating me. There is no hierarchy. I've been here longer than her yet that brings no privileges. We are, after all one and the same. We are all Moira. I suspect, though, that the real Moira does not have to queue to wash out her tights. She most likely has her own washing machine in the flat she shares with no one, except the occasional overnight lover. I wonder what that feels like? If her lover has clones, can't they become our lovers?

As I wait for M27 to finish I try to picture him. He'd be taller than us, of course. Maybe also a little older. He'd have dark wavy hair and brown eyes. I close my eyes and imagine him caressing me. Would the real one be sexier than the clones? Would the real lover notice if it was one of us rather than her?

M27 has finished at last. She takes the plug out of the wash basin. The water swirls and sucks out. She squeezes the water out of the tights. Her hands go pink. She catches my eye as she walks back towards dormitory. She doesn't smile but I feel her thinking. *This will be your fate too. This is our fate.*

As I start my washing I can feel M3 watching me. She's one of the oldest clones. Yet we all look the same. We're all synced to age with Moira. She can stare at me as much as she likes. She's not superior to me just because she's been around longer.

16

I move out of her way slowly. She probably knows I'm doing it deliberately. After all, she is me and I am she.

M24 is lying on her bed when I get back to the room I share with her and two others.

"I wonder what they'll give us today."

"The usual Tuesday muck," I suggest. It's always fish pie on a Tuesday. It doesn't taste of much except occasionally when they use bad fish. Then if you're wise you don't eat it.

M24 shakes her head. What, have I got it wrong? It's easily done. They tend to give us just one of Moira's tasks. It's cheaper. Of course we're all capable of doing all of them, for we are all Moira. Even Moira had to learn, though. I've been on target updates for a month now. This involves rather tedious work on an unwieldy spreadsheet. The days melt into weeks and the weeks into months.

M24 grins. "It's our birthday today." It is indeed. Moira normally does something and there's usually a small gift for each clone. Her fortieth, three years ago, was splendid. There was dancing and champagne. Enough men were invited so that each girl had a dancing partner for the whole evening. None of them were clones of the man on her arm. They were all human originals. And we each received a slim silver chain, the only luxury item we possess.

Moira is already in the dining room as we file in. She is dressed in a simple green dress, one that looks as if it is made of silk. It goes well with our red hair. There's never any silk for us though, just cotton if we're lucky but more usually something synthetic and uncomfortable. At least, though, tonight we should be fed properly. They're always a little concerned about our weight. We're a little sedentary compared with the real Moira. She certainly can't afford a gym membership for all of us. So, they're mean with the food on ordinary days. Not today, though, we hope.

"Ladies, please be seated." As we sit down she remains standing. She smiles at us. We understand that smile only too well. It means she is about to play with us just as she does with the officers. "This birthday my gift to you will be an opportunity. Each girl will have the same chance though only one can be successful." She pauses and grins again. "Even Clone M59 is invited to join in. Be kind to her, ladies."

As usual she marks her birthday by commissioning a new clone. The new girl walks on to the small stage. We all clap her. We daren't not. Of course she looks just like all of us, and like Moira. Just as mature as well. Yet there is a freshness about her and almost an innocence. I swear she blushes a little as she makes her way to join her table. Well, she'll know less than the rest of us, but she'll also perhaps be more enthusiastic and have a little more energy. Even though she's been synced she is really younger.

"Enjoy your meal," says Moira. "Don't worry about the challenge. All will be revealed as time goes by."

It's a good meal: smoked salmon, roast lamb, lemon mousse and a good red wine. Yet we hardly notice for the conversation is intense. Why is she giving up? Why retire so young? Are we ill? Which clone will be chosen to be human?

The conversations continue into the night. We talk for hours in our room and we can also hear the murmurings from the other rooms.

An officer shouts, "Enough ladies. Quiet now. Work tomorrow."

We all sleep eventually. And of course, the next day is just another day.

Life goes on as drably as usual. We almost forget about the challenge. We even forget to try and figure out what it might be. I ask myself if I want to become the real Moira. It would mean more freedom, yes, but also more responsibilities. I worry though about why she is giving up so soon.

M59 is assigned to help me with the spreadsheets. She learns quickly. As you would expect. We are quick learners.

"It's got too many macros," she says. "And you shouldn't use a spreadsheet for what is basically text."

I entirely agree. No surprises there. Except it is surprising that Moira has allowed this. It must be that she doesn't know this particular process so well.

I find that I like M59 much more than some of the other Moiras. This puzzles me. We are all the same aren't we?

As we queue one evening to wash out our tights M32 attacks me. "You're showing favouritism to a sister clone. You're not supposed to."

I shrug my shoulders. "I don't understand it either. Maybe I'm becoming human." She goes to strike me but fortunately – or perhaps unfortunately – for it is sure to set the other woman against me – an officer steps in and holds her back.

"I think you are," whispers M59. "You are very human. Or, at least, humane."

"Don't talk like that," I say. "It could be dangerous."

A few more weeks pass and M59 develops an illness. That isn't supposed to happen. Why haven't the normal health programmes worked on her? Perhaps she is The One. She is so sick that she must stay in bed for a week. I bring her bouquets of wild flowers from our allotments and I make her herbal teas.

"There," she says as she begins to get better. "I told you you were becoming human."

I shudder at the thought of what might happen if we're overheard. I know they're listening all the time anyway. I try to shush her.

19

The door bursts open and I'm not surprised.

I am startled, though, to see, or rather to smell, that it is the real Moira. Unmistakably. It's her perfume. We never manage to get any perfume. Well, except when we did one birthday. Then it was the cheap kind and not the designer version she always wears. We all put it on every day but actually after the first day or two we didn't notice it anymore. We all smelt the same. And because it was cheap it faded quickly. Moira grins at us and we smile back. "Well done 27. You have shown that you have some humanity." She nods at 59, who claps and shouts, "There, I told you so."

So I've now been living with Moira for six weeks. We share a bottle of Merlot sitting on the balcony, watching the city relax into the evening. We've worked hard today. We've achieved a lot. We deserve this. Though we probably haven't worked as hard as the clones and they're probably not relaxing yet.

She gives me our slow mysterious smile. I brace myself for a puzzle. "It's time," she says. "I'm leaving tomorrow."

"Where will you go?"

"I'm going to live by the sea. I've bought a small holiday home in a warm country."

"But why do you have to go? So soon?"

"I have a defective heart. They can't grow a new one in time."

"But the clones?"

She misunderstands my question. She rubs my arm. "Don't forget you are actually considerably younger than me. You have thousands of heart beats left yet. Millions."

No, we would never take a life to save our own. How could I ever suggest it?

"There's time for them to do some more research. They

20

can stop it affecting new clones. They've already starting growing you another heart. You'll be able to live at the seaside too but hopefully you'll have to wait until you're an old lady."

"And the others?"

She shrugs and shakes her head. Her eyes look sad. Well, of course not. There'd never be enough funds for that.

I become Moira. I work hard and I work smartly. I take on her lover and he doesn't notice the difference. I don't love him. Did she? I somehow doubt it. My goodness, though, the sex is good. The first time I was a little afraid. "It was so charming," he whispers into my hair, "the way you acted so virginal. Please do it again. It really turns me on."

I can't oblige. Within days, though, I acquire her sexual prowess. We are surely both in this relationship just for the sex. He seems happy enough to continue this way. It suits me too. I savour his body but I don't want his soul.

I enjoy our apartment, our wardrobe and our life style. And our money, naturally.

I hope for the new heart and occasionally ask our handler for an update on its progress.

Six months pass and I am still going to the gym every day. That is what we do. Except the clones don't get the chance. But it is in our nature. Today is no exception. I go on the cross skier, the rower and the stepper. I lift some weights and then swim twenty lengths.

I do everything as enthusiastically as usual but it's not as liberating as it should be. I feel tired today. I'm breathless as I shower. I give the sauna a miss. I sit in the changing room trying to get my breath. A young woman asks me if I'm all right. I want to be but I know I'm not. I manage to get my medicare card out of my bag and hand it to her.

She reads it quickly and almost understands. "Shall I call them?"

I nod. I have no breath to speak. As she phones the pain starts. It seems to go from my throat all over my left side. I've never felt pain like it. I've never been ill before, though I have dropped the odd file on my toe or walked into the corner of a desk. That has hurt but it's never been like this.

I'm vaguely aware of one of the trainers trying to administer first aid. I'm still conscious when the paramedics arrive. They give me something for the pain and I'm comfortable again. But I can feel my heart failing.

As they carry me into the ambulance I think of Moira. She posted pictures yesterday on Clonenet. Life beside the sea seems to suit her. I guess I'm never going to see the sea now. The new heart won't be ready in time. I wonder who will replace me and hope that it will be M59.

The Truth about Old Fuzzy Locks

Oh no. It looked as if they were on the move again.

The edges of the Grotto were beginning to blur. There had been cornfields and orchards around them yesterday. And for several weeks before that. Proper English countryside. Now there were the all too familiar rainbow streaks, which mean that they were once more hurtling through time and space to a new destination.

Perhaps that's why it was hot. Perhaps they were going somewhere warmer.

A pity. Martin liked it here. He knew that his ma and pa liked it there as well.

The rainbow swirls at the edge of the Grotto gradually disappeared.

He didn't know whether he should go and look or whether he ought to get back.

Why did he always get so scared? He ought to be used to it by now.

No, Well I'm going anyway, thought Martin. He pushed a rock under the barrel he'd been moving to stop it rolling away. And he set off towards the edge of the Grotto.

He found himself standing on a narrow ledge. He could see for miles – over what looked like snow-covered mountains. And curiously it was just as warm here as in the Grotto. Down below was a lake, filled with milky blue water, not like any other water he had seen before.

This was a new one. Well, you've got to give him that. Still finding new places to send us, even after five hundred years.

Suddenly, he thought he heard somebody coming. His eyes grew as wide as pizza.

He ought not to be scared, really. If it was a Homeling

and it got into the Grotto, it might take a year off their time – especially if they can help it to get out.

Martin could not believe his eyes. It was only Old Fuzzy Locks, the apology for a wizard. How could he be scared of him? But there was someone – or something else with him.

He watched the figure that was making its way with the tatty wizard into the Grotto. It was smaller even than him. Martin couldn't help but envy its smooth skin. He may be still a child himself, and still have to do what his parents said, but five hundred years in the Grotto had made his skin as hard as leather. He put a hand up to his face and felt the crinkles.

Don't come here, he thought. *You might never get back home. You might become one of us.*

The creature had long, droopy ears and fine pointed fingers. Its eyes were as blue and as milky as the lake down below. Its arms and legs were bare and it was wearing a gold-coloured tunic. He couldn't tell whether it was a boy or girl.

But he didn't really care all that much. He was torn between wanting the creature to stay, fulfil a quest and shorten their time in the Grotto, and wanting him to go safely back to its own world. Because Fuzzy Locks had told them time and time again that something horrible happened to the unsuccessful Homelings.

There was a sudden bang and a flash. A cloud of smoke hovered in the air and next to it, not in it, like he was supposed to arrive, Old Fuzzy Locks appeared. He looked worse than ever today. There were great tears in his robes. His hat drooped carelessly from his head. His magic wand was broken, and Martin had the distinct impression that the rather nasty smell he had suddenly become aware of was in fact coming from the old wizard.

Suddenly he wanted to get out of there. He wanted to go home and tell them all that a new Homeling had arrived. But he just had to watch what was happening. He had never been there before when a Homeling arrived and had its first meeting with the wizard. He just might learn something.

He was a little too far away from the wizard and the strange creature to hear what they were saying. But he watched anyway. The wizard turned round and started to make his way out of the Grotto. The Homeling followed.

Should he follow them and see what they did? But what if the Grotto moved on while he was out there? He'd never get back home then.

Martin shrugged. Perhaps if they ever did get back or settled down in one time or place, one of the first things he might do was find a few new friends. Oh, he liked all his friends in the Grotto, especially his best friend, Piet. But he did get bored sometimes.

Suddenly the strange creature and the smelly old wizard disappeared from in front of him. All he could see now was the edge of the Grotto and the beginning of the new land.

That decided it. He was going.

Soon he was walking along the narrow ledge. He didn't want to look down. There was nothing between them and the odd looking liquid except a few bits of jagged rock and lots and lots of space. He had no idea what the pale blue stuff was and the mountain looked as if it was made out of sharp glass.

The wizard stopped suddenly, just in front of him. He said something to the Homeling who suddenly jumped off the side of the mountain.

Martin gasped and put his hand in front of his mouth. But instead of falling and being smashed to pieces by the sharp rocks, or drowning in the lake, the Homeling flew up into the air and sped out of sight. He could fly. Martin wished he could do that.

He heard a door slam. He turned to see where the noise had come from.

That must be where he lived. It was a scruffy-looking little cottage. Scruff Locks had brought them to his own world. But why?

Could it be a trick? Oh, he just didn't care. He was along the ledge in seconds not daring to think of what would happen if his foot slipped.

He stared at the front door. The windows were covered in thick dust and the bottom frame of the door had broken away.

"Home of Alphanosa Omegatoris," he read out aloud. "Illustrious Member of the League Wizards. Knock once if you are of the magic order. Twice if not."

Should he knock? Who the heck is Alphanosa Omegatoris in any case? It certainly wasn't Fuzzy Locks. He couldn't be an illustrious member of anything. He must be just visiting.

He heard someone cough.

Should he make a move now, while he still could?

There was another cough.

Martin wanted to move but he couldn't.

There was another loud cough, followed by a sneeze.

Yes, he'd better go. He started to run. But then he didn't know what was the scariest – meeting this Alpha… Omy… whatever or falling from the ledge which seemed even narrower now. He could fall at any second.

A couple of times, he felt himself stumble but was relieved when his feet landed back on the path but he couldn't help feeling curious about this Alphy… Omy… whatever.

He was still cursing himself two days later. Why had he

chickened out like that? He'd had a real chance to find out more about that old plonker and he'd blown it.

That Alpha... Omy... whatsity, though. He might be a thousand times cleverer than Old Fuzzy Locks. And he might get stuck outside the Grotto, if he went poking around there again.

He decided then. He'd rather that happened than never know, and live on for goodness knows how much longer, knowing that he had had the chance to find out something more and never took it. And he knew Fuzzy Locks wasn't there. Because he was in the Grotto having tea with Ma and Pa.

Martin placed his cap firmly on his head. And he was off. Striding out of the Grotto, feeling really pleased with himself.

It was strange, this place. He was high up in the mountains. And it looked cold out there, everywhere blue and white as if covered in snow. But it wasn't cold at all. It was so hot he needed a sun hat.

It was so good to get out of the Grotto. The ledge didn't scare him so much this time. And gradually it even became fun. In fact, it was quite an adventure. And in no time at all, he was standing outside the little cottage again.

He would ring twice. Whoever lived here might be able to tell him something about Old Fuzzy Locks. He might even be able to help them.

He hesitated for a second and then pulled the handle on the bell twice. He waited. His heart was thumping against his rib cage. But nothing happened. No illustrious wizard came rushing to the door. No one cast a spell on him.

This was no good. He couldn't just go back and tell Piet he hadn't found a thing. He pushed at the door. It wasn't locked and it opened easily. Martin walked in as quietly as he could.

It was really gloomy inside. No matter how bright the sun was, it just could not get in through the dust on the windows.

But his eyes did gradually get used to the dark. Enough for him to see just how untidy the cottage was. There were papers all over the floor and more papers and books piled high on a heavy wooden desk. There was a nasty smell coming from somewhere. It became stronger as Martin moved round the room towards the fireplace. Then he saw it. On a small table next to the big armchair near the fire was a mouldy piece of cheese. It smelt so horrible he thought he was going to be sick.

But he wasn't. Seconds later a scrabbling noise was coming from under the armchair. Then came some squeaking. And finally growling.

Suddenly a blob of black fur flew through the air and thudded on the ground.

"Tabatha!" cried Martin. He would recognise those evil eyes anywhere. She must be the biggest, ugliest cat that ever existed. There couldn't be more than one like her. So, Fuzzy Locks must be here after all. Tabatha was his cat.

The animal darted towards the door, the mouse now dead, hanging from its mouth. It glowered at Martin, as if to say "You keep away. This is all mine."

"Yes, you take that outside then," said Martin to the big cat, as he opened the door. "Don't you dare start crunching it in front of me."

The cat seemed to scowl at him, and then it pushed past him and rushed out. A breeze came in and blew some of the papers off the table on to the floor. Martin went to pick them up. Light was now coming into the room. He couldn't help noticing that the two pieces of paper were really thick and the print was really elegant. They looked really important. He should put them back carefully, really. But he couldn't

28

resist taking a look. '*Head Office, League of Wizards, Missive to Alphanosa Omegatoris*' read Martin. This was something else. He carried on reading.

Dear Mr Omegatoris,
  Whilst the conjuring trick of sending the Lombardy Grotto and the inhabitants thereof to alternative places and times would be admirable in a junior or trainee wizard, it is hardly impressive in one of your experience and standing. Apart from how cruel it is to the inhabitants of the Grotto. We therefore regret to inform you that not only can we not admit you to the Guild of Master Wizards, but also that your membership of the League of Wizards is suspended.

Yours faithfully,
Olando Bericha

So this **was** where Old Fuzzy Locks lived. Fuzzy Locks was Alpha whatsity.

The second piece of paper had the same heading.

'*Dear Mr Omegatoris,*' read Martin.

  We are still not satisfied with your performance as a wizard. So, we have decided to issue you with a Direct Challenge. Any of the so-called Homelings who fail in the quests you set them will be suspended in polycubes. They will not suffer, and neither will the Lombarders any more than they do already. You will need to use the three rules of magic to the utmost of their power.
  Your suspension from the League of Wizards will remain in force until such time as all Homelings are freed. However, if you succeed in freeing all Homelings at a stroke, you will be reinstated and promoted to Master Wizard.

A word of caution. This will not be easy. The more you fail, the harder it will get, and the less faith you will have in yourself. But remember, we would not have set you this challenge, unless we thought you could do it. Good luck.

Yours sincerely,
The Wizard Master.

So, Old Fuzzy Locks was more than just a scruffy old idiot, after all. But what on earth was a polycube?

Martin didn't have time to wonder for long. He suddenly heard footsteps outside. He stuffed the letters in his pocket and hid behind the armchair.

The footsteps got nearer. The door cracked open a little more. Martin watched a dark shape move into the room.

Well, it didn't look or smell like Old Fuzzy Locks.

The shape moved slowly towards him. Martin held his breath. Whoever it was stopped and looked around, and then started treading carefully between the piles of paper.

"Martin, are you there?" whispered a voice. It was Piet. Martin came out from behind the armchair.

"Well, I'm glad you're all right," said Piet. "I really couldn't work out what you were up to. I just had to follow you. You're a prize idiot. The Grotto could move again, at any minute. Then where would you be? You're too daft by half, you are. That's your trouble."

Martin decided to ignore him.

"It's a good job I did come here," said Martin. "You should see what I've found out."

Martin showed his friend the two letters. They sat outside. They knew that Fuzzy Locks wouldn't be back for at least another two hours.

It was a change for them, looking at a different view. In the Grotto, they had to look at the same old things all the time.

"So I wonder where these polycube things are?" said Piet.

"Who knows?" said Martin. "But one thing's for sure; he ain't such an idiot as we thought. He just acts that way."

"He certainly does that," said Piet.

"I suppose we'd better stop calling him Old Fuzzy Locks," said Martin. "His real name's Alpha..." He looked down at the letter.

Piet looked over his shoulder.

"Why don't we call him Alpha Omy for short?" suggested Piet.

It seemed a good idea. But Martin didn't have chance to think about it much. Piet was suddenly shaking his arm and screaming.

"Oh no, look at that will you?" He was pointing towards the Grotto. The edges were beginning to blur and the rainbow colours were beginning to form. "It's going," he said. "It's off again already."

They ran. They ran as fast as they could. They hardly worried about the narrowness of the ledge along which Martin had walked so carefully just a few days before. Their sides were aching and they were out of breath. But still they ran.

The Grotto was beginning to spin and the rainbow colours were getting brighter and brighter.

"We're not going to make it," panted Piet.

"We will," answered Martin. "Step on it."

They stepped on it.

Martin actually had his foot on the pathway of the Grotto when suddenly it wasn't there anymore.

"Now look!" moaned Piet. "I told you we shouldn't have come. I told you this would happen."

But something didn't quite make sense to Martin. If the Grotto had moved on, it had done so with Fuzzy Locks, or

31

Alpha Omy even, in it. And Alpha Omy was often in the Grotto. So there must be a direct link between the Grotto and here.

"But I don't get it," said Martin. "We know Fuzzy Locks is in the Grotto."

"Well, it's magic, isn't it?" said Piet.

"Yeah, but why bother with magic, when he could have just walked home?" replied Martin.

"So, who cares?" asked Piet. "What are **we** going to do now?"

"We could go and explore," said Martin.

"And get into even more trouble?" asked Piet.

"Well, just for a couple of hours," answered Martin. "We know he's leaving the Grotto then. Perhaps he'll come back home and perhaps he'll be able to help us get back."

"Him? Be helpful?" asked Piet. "That's not very likely, is it?"

"Well, what do you suggest?" asked Martin. He couldn't keep the sharp tone out of his voice. Piet was being such a misery again.

Piet shrugged his shoulders.

"Just think," he said. "We could have been sitting at home, getting ready for our dinner, if we hadn't gone chasing Old Fuzzy Locks."

But they weren't at home. They were here. Didn't Piet get that?

Martin looked around him. Now that the Grotto had gone, there was nothing but the blue white of the mountains and the milky lake below. There was no sound at all. Certainly no more sign of the Homeling they had seen or of any of the others who lived here.

"I wonder where he went," said Martin.

Piet shrugged his shoulders again. "I hope he hasn't gone into one of those polycubes."

"Well, I'm going to have a look down there, anyway," said Martin. He set off down the path which would have lead him into the Grotto if it had still been there. Piet followed him. Martin could tell he was unhappy. He was always a pace or two behind, and he seemed to be dragging his feet along the ground.

In the end, there was nothing much to see. It was all so empty. It was funny how they spent all that time wanting to get out of the Grotto, and when they were out, it was boring.

"Alright," he said. "Let's go back to his place."

They walked back up. Martin kicked at the ground. This was such a good opportunity to find out more about the wizard, and yes, the letters had been a good find, but there had been nothing more since.

Piet stopped suddenly.

"What if he won't help us though?" he said. "Or can't."

It was Martin's turn to shrug. He really had no idea what they would do if the wizard wouldn't or couldn't help them.

They had almost got to the cottage when there was a sudden loud bang. A cloud of smoke hung in the air. Seconds later the wizard appeared. Next to the cloud, not in it. And then there was that strange smell that always came with Fuzzy Locks nowadays.

"He's definitely still Fuzzy Locks today then," said ed Piet. "Just look at him will you?"

The wizard's beard looked greyer and untidier than ever. His robe was even more torn. His hat drooped so much now that it seemed to be actively looking for something on the ground.

"I can't even get that right these days," he was muttering to himself. He opened the door and let himself in. Then he slammed the door hard.

"I think you're right," said Martin, and suddenly both boys were laughing helplessly.

33

"Come on," said Martin, when at last they had calmed down, "let's go and see what he's up to."

Piet did not complain this time, but just followed. Martin pushed open the door of the cottage. His eyes adjusted quickly to the dark. It seemed to be completely empty.

"Where's he got to then?" asked Piet. "Are there any more rooms here or what?"

Martin didn't know. But it looked unlikely.

"I'm sure it's just this room. If you think about how big it seems from outside…"

He carried on looking round the untidy little room. There were no doors. Except the one to what he assumed was a cupboard bed. Well, even wizards had to sleep somewhere didn't they?

"What's in here then?" asked Piet, looking at the same door.

"His bed?" suggested Martin.

"Perhaps he's having a snooze," said Piet.

"Open it and have a look then," said Martin.

"No, you," said Piet, standing there with his arms folded.

Martin went to open the door to the cupboard. But as his hand rested on the handle, the ground moved from beneath his feet. He was twirling round and round in the air. The same rainbows which swirled round the Grotto when it moved were spinning around him now, only brighter and faster. There was a faint smell of ripe peaches.

He was aware of a shadow turning round at his side. Was it Piet? He was moving much too fast to be able to tell for sure. But then the shadow spoke.

"What's going on then?" said Piet's voice. "What's he done now?"

Suddenly they landed roughly on the ground. They

were no longer in Old Fuzzy Lock's cottage. Nor were they back in the Grotto. They were in a big hall with a high roof and a shiny wooden floor. And lined up in front of them were row upon row of large cubes. In each cube was a person or a creature, caught forever in the middle of an action.

"The polycubes," said Martin. "These must be the polycubes."

"Oh heck," said Piet, "how has he managed that?"

The two boys started to wander along the lines of polycubes. There was such an odd collection of different people. There was even a bear in one of them. Martin bit his lip when they came across the little creature they had seen talking to the wizard two days ago. It seemed to be looking at something behind Martin and was pointing with his elegant finger towards the sky. So, that Homeling hadn't made it then.

"I wouldn't mind getting to know them," said Piet. He was looking at two polycubes, one with a boy in and the other a girl. They looked about the same age as Martin and Piet. Without the leathery skin, of course. Their clothes were made out of shiny metal. The boy was jumping, almost flying, and the girl looked as if she was swimming upwards through the air. "I wonder where they come from?" he added.

But Martin was beginning to feel uncomfortable.

"This is really horrid," he said to Piet. "It's as if they're in an exhibition."

"Yeah," agreed Piet, "but it shows he's cleverer than we thought."

Martin wanted to protest that it wasn't clever. That it would really be clever if the old fraud did something about it and let all those people out. He opened his mouth ready to speak, when they suddenly heard a loud cough.

"So, we have a couple of Lombarders escaped have we?" said a familiar voice. Old Fuzzy Locks was standing in front of them. He looked as tatty as ever, but he was standing up a bit taller. "You always read other people's mail do you, then?" he asked looking straight at Martin.

Martin felt himself blush. He went to say something.

"You think it's alright, do you," the wizard continued, "just to walk into somebody's home, without as much as knocking?"

Martin tried to think of a reply, but he couldn't. He blushed even deeper.

"Anyway, it doesn't matter," said the Wizard. "You know, don't you, that I've got a big job on here?"

Martin nodded.

"You do see don't you, that there's more to all this than me just playing tricks on you and the other Lombarders?"

Martin nodded again.

"And you know I've got to use the three rules of magic?" The wizard sat down suddenly on the little wooden bench at the side of the hall. He sighed. "The trouble is," he said, "I've lost the knack with the first one."

Martin noticed his that Piet was staring at the wizard. He was frowning slightly, but for once he was standing up straight and not trying to hide.

"Well what's that?" asked Piet. There was a slight tremble in his voice, but at least he was speaking.

The wizard sighed again. "It's about having faith. About having the faith that you can do it. The trouble is, the more I can't do it, the harder it gets to have faith."

Martin remembered the letter from the Guild of Wizards.

"Look at me," said Alpha Omy. He held up his arms to show them just exactly how bad his robes had become. The whole of one sleeve had worn away underneath. "I'm not even allowed to go shopping any more. Nor go to the conferences to find out the latest new ideas. And how I used to think I knew it all when I was your age!"

"Oh get a grip!" said Piet. Martin couldn't quite take this in. His moany wimpy friend was telling the moany wimpy wizard what to do. Piet took hold of the wizard's arm and marched him over to the polycube with the long fingered creature in it. He was really walking tall now.

Martin's mouth dropped open. He was truly amazed.

"Just look at that will you?" shouted Piet. He was really getting into this now. "How can you let that carry on? Do something."

"Oh but I can't. I've tried, but I can't," whimpered the wizard.

"Well you're going to have to," said Piet. Martin's mouth dropped open even further as he saw his friend push the wizard right up to the polycube. He had to smile though, when he noticed how pale Piet had gone and that he was shaking.

"How would you like if that happened to you?" he said.

"Well, something bad has happened to me. Look at me!"

"A few tatty clothes," said Piet, "kicked out of the League of Wizards for a bit. That's nothing!"

Martin wanted to join in. But he was so amazed at how bold his friend had suddenly become, that he couldn't think what to say.

"Well, go on then," said Piet. "Do something." He sat down next to the wizard, who looked even paler now.

The old man hesitated for a moment. He frowned.

"I can't," he said.

"You can," said Piet. His little outburst seemed to be sapping away all of his strength.

The wizard sighed again. Then he took a deep breath.

He pulled himself up tall and pointed at the cube.

Martin felt a little light-headed. The air around him was vibrating gently. He and Piet stared at the polycube. Nothing seemed to happen.

"It's no good," said the Wizard. "I've definitely lost the knack." He sat down on the bench again.

"So what do you have to do?" asked Piet. He had gone quite pale. His voice was definitely back to normal now. Frightened and squeaky.

"You just have to have faith that you can do it," said the old man. "Only I haven't got any left."

Martin stared at the creature in the polycube. It was just a matter of believing that you could free him? Make all that funny solid see-though stuff go away? Suddenly he felt as if he was filling up with some sort of energy. There was a real warm glow inside him. He felt as if he was growing taller and taller. The air was really humming now, and he could hear a thousand or more voices whispering. "Have faith. You can do it."

He carried on staring at the trapped creature. *I really can get you out of there,* he thought. *It's down to me. I've got to do it and I can do it.*

Martin's hand floated up. No matter what he did, he couldn't make it come back down to his side. A hot rush of pins and needles came down from his shoulder and a flash came from the end of his finger. It went towards the creature. This was it. He knew he was going to make a difference.

The heat drained out of Martin and he felt himself go back to his normal size. For a few seconds, there was a sharp pain in his head and he thought he was going to be sick. Then it passed.

Suddenly the creature's arm which was pointing upwards floated down to its side. There were bubbles inside the cube.

"It's turned into liquid," said Piet, who seemed not to have noticed the strange things which had been happening to Martin.

"Yes," said Alpha Omy. There seemed to be no strength in him. "I remembered how I used to be when I was your age. Dead cocky and nothing could go wrong. Well done, young man," he continued, looking at Martin now. "You've discovered – and used rather successfully – the first rule of magic."

"So what will happen next?" asked Martin.

"I guess I'll have to use the second rule of magic to turn the cube into air and then the third to break open the cube," he answered. "But it will take some time. And then there's all the others. Perhaps you'll come back and help me sometime?"

"How many are there?" asked Martin.

"Two thousand exactly," replied the wizard.

"Ooh," moaned Piet.

"But at least we've made a start," said the wizard.

"So what are the other two rules of magic?" asked Martin. Could he learn to be a wizard as well? He'd like to be a really good one and join the Guild of Master Wizards.

Alpha Omy stood up.

"Anything is possible," he said, as if he could read Martin's thoughts.

"But I'm not giving all of my secrets away in one go," he said. "And you boys must get back to the Grotto. Not a word about this to anyone mind, or," he leant over and looked straight into Martin's eyes, "or I'll turn you both into frogs. And I can, you know."

Alpha Omy laughed until his laugh became a roar. He waved the tatty bent stick he called his magic wand at them. Soon came the rainbow colours again and they were whirling faster and faster through space. Seconds later they were standing outside the cave where Piet lived.

"Not bad for someone who's been chucked out of the League of Wizards," commented Piet.

"And where do you think you two have been?" screeched an angry voice. Piet's ma was standing at the entrance to her cave with one hand on her hip. "Your dinner's getting cold."

"We've been talking to Alpha Omy," stammered Piet.

"Who?" boomed Mrs Lintern.

"Alpha Omy," repeated Piet. "You know, Old Fuzzy Locks."

"Oh, him," said Mrs Lintern, calming down a little. "He ought to know better than to keep you talking at dinner time."

"Well, he's cleverer than what you think, Ma," said Piet. "And he's got to get the Homelings out of the polycubes."

"Oh for goodness sake," muttered Martin. "Keep your mouth shut."

"Are you all right boy?" asked Mrs Lintern, suddenly looking worried. She put her hand out to feel Piet's forehead. "Well, you don't seem to have a temperature. But maybe I'd better give you a dose of feverfew anyway. Get yourself inside!"

"But Ma," protested Piet. "His name's really Alpha Omy and he's not such an idiot as you think!"

"Come on, son," said Mrs Lintern, more gently now "the feverfew will help." She turned to Martin. "You'd better get home, as well, my dear. Your parents will be worried, what with the Grotto moving and all."

Martin nodded at Mrs Lintern. Piet scowled at him. Martin had to move quickly before he started to giggle. Feverfew! Gross. But it served him right for opening his big mouth.

Martin stared out past the edge of the Grotto. They were by the sea now. The light of the setting sun was catching the heads of the waves.

They were pink ponies, not white horses. That looked like another good place to explore. Maybe he'd actually miss going to different places if the Grotto did settle down one day.

Water

Carl turned on the tap that would allow water into the levies running through the cabbage fields. It shouldn't be a problem. There'd been plenty of rain earlier in the year and anyway, they were still connected to the main grid. Ever since everything had settled down after the Changes, there had never been any problem with the water supply. Someone was still managing the big reservoirs, so it seemed, and the climate, despite the predictions of the previous century, was behaving well. The cycles of winter and summer, cold and heat, rain and sunshine, and all that they brought, had carried on just as before.

It was hot, now, though and it had been pretty dry for the last six weeks. All the crops had to be watered, clearly, but the cabbage was now particularly important. Deprive it of water now and they might lose all of it.

Carl pushed back his base-ball cap and wiped the sweat from his forehead. Any second now he would hear the gurgle that told him the water had arrived in the pipe, and the woosh-woosh as the levy filled. He could imagine himself putting his hand into the cool water, cupping it, and taking a welcome drink. So, what if irrigation water wasn't recommended? He'd been drinking it for years and had never had any ill effect. What usually took seconds seemed to be taking hours, though, today. Carl shut his eyes and waited.

There was suddenly a loud clunk and the pipe leading up to the tap began to hum.

"What the blazes…?" said Carl to no one in particular.

Carl sat in the Great Hall fanning his face with his hat. The air con units still worked but they were used sparingly: since the Changes – energy as well as water was precious.

"So you tested the whole network?" said the senior Proctor. "And there was no sign of a leak anywhere?"

"Nope!" said Carl. He had checked. Absolutely thoroughly. Not that he'd needed to. He and Barnaby always kept the pipes in excellent order. "The leak must be before it gets to us," he said. "Or else it's a problem with the reservoir."

"Very well," said the Proctor. "I'll send a team to investigate. I'd like you or Barnaby Jackson to head the team. Not both of you."

It would be the first time anyone had left the Compound in over five years. The last time had been when they'd buried those that had died of the mystery illness. They'd gone as far away from the survivors as they could without putting their lives at risk in other ways. The reservoir was at least a week's journey away, if they kept stopping to listen for leaks.

Carl nodded and left the Hall. The coolness of the dark corridors outside was welcome. It didn't make him feel any more comfortable, though. Now he had to go and have a difficult conversation with Barnaby Jackson. Yet, he felt strangely excited.

Carl stared at the great expanse of water that stretched in front of him. He hadn't realised the reservoir would be so big. It looked still and calm but the breeze was enough to make small waves ripple at its edges. It matched the turquoise of the sky. Where the sides weren't built up there were sandy beaches. He suddenly had a longing for the days when people took leisure trips to places such as this. Families having picnics by the side of the water. Kids swimming and young men diving off the rocks. Older guys like him fishing or perhaps taking a boat across.

There was no time for that sort of thing these days. They only survived if they worked.

"Well, there's nothing wrong with that," said Patrick O'Leary. He was pointing to the high water mark. It was only about a foot above where the water was now. "There must be something blocking it up right here," he said. All of the pipes they'd listened to had been totally empty.

Carl nodded and got down from his horse. He was saddle-sore but otherwise glad he'd come instead of Barnaby. There'd been no straw poll in the end. Barnaby had a wife and three daughters. Carl was single. It had been a no-brainer. And it had all been worth it. They'd seen plenty of water on the way. There were lots of other supplies they could use if there was something wrong with the reservoir, though it would mean piping them. He'd been overwhelmed, too, by the richness of the scenery; the lakes and streams, obviously, but the pine forests with the deep blue sky setting off their dark green needles, and the mountains in the distance, terracotta fingers, nails lacquered with snow. He knew he would have to find other excuses for leaving the Compound. Now he had seen all of this, though, he could not be without it.

"So what's the plan?" said Bradley Spenser, who'd been mainly responsible for finding the way here.

"Try to find out who's been looking after this place," said Carl. "And see what's wrong. Maybe we can help."

Two hours later they had found out very little. There was a cottage where it looked as if someone had lived for a while. It was untidy and abandoned and whoever had lived there had left in a hurry. There were the maggot-infected remains of what looked like a half-eaten meal on the kitchen table. And it whiffed.

"I'm going to barf if we don't get out of here soon," said Wilf Atkins.

Yes, Carl knew what he meant. It stank. But it still

44

didn't help them to work out why the water supply had failed though the water was plentiful.

"Why don't we go for a swim and look again later?" suggested Bradley. "It'll give us a bit more energy."

Well it wouldn't hurt.

It was quite good in the end, even if it hadn't been the type of family holiday leisure day out Carl had thought about earlier. It just wasn't the same with a group of ugly middle-aged men skinny-dipping and telling dirty jokes. Still it was good to feel clean from the water and then sleepy from the sun on your back as you stretched out to dry.

Until Patrick shouted out just after he'd gone into the water for the third time. "Cripes, mate, will you look at this? Holy shit, I can't move it."

The others rushed back into the water. Patrick kept taking a deep breath and diving down. "It's a body," he said. "And it seems to be blocking up the main channel out of the reservoir. There's some sort of door down there, and it's half shut. Mates, I think we've found the problem."

It took them another hour to get the body out of the water. They were as hot and thirsty after they'd finished that as they were before they'd had their swim. They got him out at last and even managed to open the door so that the water could flow freely again.

"There must be some sort of system to that," said Bradley. "And I bet he's the only geyser who knew how it worked."

They found a set of keys in his pocket. Carl guessed they would be for the cottage and perhaps something to do with some engine room that worked on the gates of the reservoir.

Carl stared at the body. It was bloated and grey. Half of its face was missing. Eaten by fish, he supposed. Poor guy. "How long do you think he's been there?" he said.

"About a week before we lost our water supply?" suggested Bradley. "That's how long it would take the pipes to empty, I'm thinking."

That made sense, he supposed. He didn't have time to think about it for long, though. Suddenly they could hear motorbike engines.

"Where've the bastards got their fuel from?" murmured Wilf, grabbing his clothes and picking up the rifle that never left his side. It looked good but it would be useless if the visitors posed any real danger; ammunition other than blanks for it had run out more than ten years ago.

"We'd better hide," said Bradley.

Carl and Spenser picked up their clothes and followed Wilf into the bushes.

Carl watched the two riders get off their Triumphs. For a few seconds he envied them. Before the Changes he used to own a small Triumph. One of the classier ones like one of those had been next on his shopping list.

The riders took off their helmets. One of them shook out long straight hair. It looked just like the hair in one of the old shampoo ads. How did they manage to stay so well-groomed?

The strangers walked towards the water's edge and stood right in front of the bushes where the men were hiding.

"Plenty of water here," one of them said. Cripes, it was a girl.

"Shall we set up camp here, then?" the other rider replied. Another female.

The first girl turned towards where they were hiding. My god, she was gorgeous. Carl wished he could touch her. He'd not come across a woman who'd made him feel like that in a long, long time. He mouth was dry and his heart was pounding. And for the first time in months he was getting an erection that he hadn't induced himself. She was so close now. It was unbearable. He turned so the others couldn't see; there had been no time to dress.

Atkins fired his rifle into the air. The plainer of the two girls shrieked. Then both of them ran towards their bikes. Seconds later they were riding back towards the road. Carl's erection collapsed.

What had he gone and done that for? They could have got to know the girls, maybe invited them back to the Compound. They'd surely make good breeding stock? It was getting a bit critical back there. A shadow of the erection returned. He wouldn't mind being involved in that particular programme. Not if that girl was one of the females.

All at once, though, he couldn't move. Cripes, this hadn't happened since before the Changes. It was a rare form of epilepsy, the doctors had said. They'd given him some medication that kept it under control. Of course that ran out shortly after the troubles started. But he'd never had another attack, and he guessed it was because life was actually even less stressful once everything had settled down than it had been before it all kicked off. He felt himself topple to the ground.

"God almighty, Carl," he heard Wilf say. "What's up?"

Bradley felt his pulse and then put his ear to his chest. "Nothing," he said. "I think he's gone."

He was still breathing and he did still have a pulse, though both would be very hard to track without a stethoscope. He could hear and see but he couldn't move a muscle. Why didn't they get a mirror to check his breathing?

"Poor bugger," said Wilf.

"Quite a nice way to go, though," said Bradley.

I'm not dead, you clots, thought Carl. *Don't you dare try to put me six foot under.*

47

"Hey," laughed Wilf, "you don't think it was because he got a bit too excited about that one with the blond hair, do you? I'd swear he's still got a bit of a stiffy."

"Oh, come on, mate," said Bradley. "You shouldn't joke about the dead. We'd better do something about these two."

Fortunately, it was too hot for the men to do more than just dig two very shallow graves, put the two bodies in and cover them with leaves. Carl could still breathe. It was just a matter of waiting.

Six hours had gone by, Carl reckoned, by the time he could move again. It was dark but at least there was a bright moon. The others had taken his clothes and his horse. His first priority was to find something to wear.

When he raided the reservoir keeper's cottage, he found that the stench that had almost made Wilf barf came not from the leftover meal but from the bodies of the woman and the baby he found upstairs.

"At least you had a woman, you lucky sod," he whispered to the reservoir keeper as he laid the woman and child to rest in what had been his own grave, "and she must have been okay to shag if you managed to impregnate her. Well, you're lying together again now. Enjoy."

He soon got the place tidied up and found out how to work the doors and gates on the reservoir. All of the machinery still worked beautifully. He smiled to himself when he thought of the folk back at the Compound amazed at how lucky they were that the reservoir was still holding out. He wondered whether they'd held a memorial service for him.

But he didn't want to try and get back. There would be too much explaining to do. Besides, it was glorious here. He could enjoy the trees against the sky and the snow-capped mountains all of the time now. The cottage was cosy and there were plenty of fish in the reservoir. If he got a bit lonely, he would go and talk to the graves of the reservoir keeper and his wife.

And who knows, one day he might hear the sound of a Triumph motorbike again. And it might even deliver a beautiful blonde woman.

The Gargoyle

"Wow!" Zizzi muttered, "even better than it looks from the computer pictures."

He had never been so impressed by any other planet he had visited. Blues, browns and green swirled around each other, tempered by white puffs of mist.

He was pleased as well with his new Ranger X57 telescope. It was so powerful, that he had been able to examine in detail this planet which had always fascinated him. And he was even more pleased with his Scout 750 Traveller which had brought him into the Earth's orbit. He would be able to take a good look now at these strange figures that adorned the grand buildings he had found out were called cathedrals. His powerful Extender computer had made a thorough analysis of the Earth language spoken in these parts and he would be able to use its translator to understand anything he read or heard. The Mentor would surely be pleased with his project. He was going to investigate why the Earthlings had representations of Zogoids – Zizzi's own race – on their churches.

The traveller was now entering the Earth's orbit. Zizzi activated the vessel's visibility shields. He stared out through the scanner screen.

Zizzi slowed the craft right down. He would have to be careful about switching from visibility shields to the chameleon drives – even the powerful Scout could not handle both at once. In the spilt second that the 750 became visible, he must make sure that no one saw him.

Zizzi smiled at the computer's choice of chameleon stance: the Scout would look like one of the strange figures he was about to investigate, and would wait on the wall of the big cathedral. He quickly flicked the visibility shield off and the chameleon mode switch on. But something was not right. He looked again at the computer screen. Oh no! Yes, the Scout looked like a gargoyle alright – the only one on the West Face!

"But perhaps no one will see," thought Zizzi. "It is dark, after all."

Dark was something Zizzi did not know on Zogo. When that planet turned away from the sun, artificial daylight flooded the living areas. Not the soft yellow light he saw now coming from the cathedral and the street lights. Zizzi decided he liked the artificial light on earth better. It was more mysterious somehow.

He watched the people going in and out of the cathedral.

"That will do," he thought. He pointed on the screen to the little girl with black curly hair. She wore a long orange scarf-come-hat, a yellow jumper and yellow tartan trousers.

Zizzi found himself at the cathedral entrance, a yellow scarf-come-hat on his head and white tartan trousers and top. "Not bad," he thought. But then he saw the boy in the striped sweatshirt, black chinos and blue deck shoes. Ooops! Then again, he had never been known for his dress sense on Zogo either.

The boy scuffed his feet along the ground as he walked. Zizzi followed him at a distance. The boy looked bored. Zizzi noticed that lots of people were avoiding walking on some of the stones on the floor that had writing on them. He caught sight of the little girl whose costume he had imitated.

"Words!" she said, pointing down at the paving-stones. "Yes," said the tall man who was holding her hand. "Those are people's graves. You should try not to walk on them." "Graves?" asked the little girl.
"Yes, where you put people who have died!"

"Oh!" The girl still looked puzzled.

Zizzi shuddered. How unhygienic! Fancy leaving dead

bodies around to rot! On Zogo, once you had stopped living, your body was annihilated. Zapped! Broken up into particles which were recycled at once. Nobody wrote messages about you on the floor!

The boy in the black chinos had his hands in his pockets. The corners of his mouth turned down. His forehead creased in the middle and two lines came up from his nose.

He looks cross, thought Zizzi.

"Look at this Gareth!" Gareth walked slowly over to where his mother was looking at a box on stilts which came almost up to her shoulders.

"St Swithun's monument. You know, if it rains on the 15th of July, it will rain for another forty days. They say it's because they buried him inside and he wanted to be buried outside!"

"That's rubbish, Mum."

Funny way to forecast the weather, thought Zizzi. *I wonder how they do it for the other 325 days?* Of course, that was why they had to put all those bodies under the floor. They hadn't learnt how to control the weather on Earth yet. So they had to know what it was going to do!

Zizzi wondered what rain felt like. It hadn't rained on Zogo for centuries. He didn't even know what water felt like. Zizzi's ancestors hadn't liked the feel of water, so they had invented a way of cleaning themselves with gentle laser guns.

Zizzi followed Mum and Gareth round the cathedral. They stopped in front of a group of statues who looked as if they were in a barn. Zizzi thought they were made of wood or stone. They looked like Earthlings, but they were shorter, although if they had been as tall, they would have been much thinner. They were a bit ugly too. But not as ugly as gargoyle or a Zogoid. And their clothes were different from those of the people walking around the cathedral. They all wore long robes which didn't look very practical. Three of them were better dressed than the others, and they wore jewels on their head. They were kneeling down looking at a baby in a primitive crib. There were animals too, less intelligent Earthlings, also staring at the baby.

Gosh! We wouldn't let the unthinking Zogoids near our newly hatched babies, thought Zizzi. *Not clean!* But he was impressed that they used straw for the baby's bedding, just like what they put the Zogoid eggs in.

"Two thousand years on and nothing's changed much!" said Mum. "Peace on Earth and good will to all men, indeed!"

"It's rubbish, Mum," said Gareth.

He's not very impressed by anything, thought Zizzi. *Perhaps he'd like it better on Zogo.* Zizzi was fascinated by the cathedral. That soft yellow light was everywhere. And those enormous arrangements of bright red flowers with their pointed leaves. On Zogo, all the plants were very pale, and you always had them to match your room exactly.

Not that Zizzi was dissatisfied with Zogo. There was always plenty to see and do, especially now that he had the new telescope and the Scout. And the Extender computer always came up with good ideas.

The Gareth and the Mum made their way towards the place Zizzi read was called the "North Transept." They were soon walking over some highly patterned tiles. Zizzi saw a notice which said that the tiles were from the thirteenth century and that visitors should take care of how they walked on them.

Better hover across, he thought. To his disgust the Gareth and the Mum just walked across normally. Zizzi hoisted himself into the air, and glided across. Something made the Gareth turn round. His mouth dropped open when he saw Zizzi suspended in the air.

"Mum!" he shouted.

"They're really beautiful, aren't they?" said Mum.

"No, but Mum…!"

It dawned on Zizzi then. Humans don't hover. He dropped to the floor at once.

"Come on," said Mum. "We'd better go and get Grandpa's present. The shop will be shut soon."

Zizzi decided to keep his distance. He looked at some of the decorations on the walls.

"I hope it's not raining. You didn't bring your coat," she continued.

Rain! He would have to see that!

Mum and Gareth were now hurrying towards the exit of the cathedral. Every now and then Gareth looked back towards Zizzi. Zizzi would not meet his eyes. He watched them from the big doorway – the West Door, he read – as they rushed across to the cathedral shop opposite. There was water falling from the sky.

Rain! Great! thought Zizzi. *I must try this!* He stepped out into the cold.

The rain was blowing towards the West Face of the cathedral. The droplets of water fell on Zizzi's hands and face. They stung. He had to close his eyes. The scarf was no protection. It only took seconds for his top to be wet through and Zizzi did not like that feeling. It was slimy, like when you touched a Zogosnail, and it was like having lots of pins stuck into you. Like grey dull metal. He felt cold and he shivered. No wonder his ancestors didn't like water. He'd had enough of rain. Should he return straight back to the Scout? But he hadn't found out any more about gargoyles yet. He looked up at the cathedral. Just one ugly face looked down at him and he knew what that was. A gust of wind pushed him towards the open door of the cathedral shop.

Yes. He would go to the shop! Perhaps he could make Mums and Gareths his project instead. And he would like to find more about that baby who had been born two thousand years ago.

Zizzi watched the shoppers. They seemed to go to a counter with the goods they wanted and then hand over some pieces of metal or a flat rectangle. The Mentor had told him about something like this on Zogo as part of a history lesson. Now if you wanted to buy something, you got the shop on the computer screen and paid for it by authorising credits with your voice. This shop was much more interesting, even if it did take much longer. It was great to be able to see the goods and even touch them.

He spotted the Gareth and the Mum by the counter.

"It's naff," said the Gareth. "But I suppose he'll like it." He was holding one of those stringy things that Zizzi had seen around the necks of some of the men in the cathedral. It was richly coloured and had pictures of those people in that barn again.

Zizzi carried on browsing. He was in the section with books. Zizzi's grandfather used to talk about books. Now the only ones you could get were those you charged up from the computer. Older people liked to read them when they were in the sleeping cells. But most Zogoids preferred to read direct from the computer. He had found some more information about the baby. It was a boy called Jesus. And he had been born in a place called Bethlehem, although his parents came from another place called Nazareth. But he couldn't find out much more from the books, because they were written for Earthlings who knew the full story.

Then he saw it. "A History of Gargoyles". The one on the cover looked just like him. And inside there were ones

55

like the Mentor, like his mother and his father, another just like his bother Tobo and even one like his pet, Horendz, with its long double ears and scaly back. He would have to buy this.

He felt in the pocket of his trousers! Yes, there were some of the strange metal Earthling coins there. He pulled them out. There were four heavy gold-coloured ones, a strange, large seven-sided silver coloured one, two smaller seven-sided silver ones and an assortment of silver and copper coloured coins, both in two different sizes. He looked at the numbers on the book. £4.99. He supposed he had enough. He would have to watch everyone very carefully at the counter.

But then the Gareth saw him.

"Eh, Mum," he said. "It's that geek again. The one who floated…"

A loud ringing noise suddenly started coming from the back of Zizzi's chameleon suit.

Zotto! he thought. *I forgot to charge the battery! I've got two minutes to get back to the ship!*

Zizzi was still clutching the book as he ran through the door of the cathedral shop.

"Hey, you haven't paid for that," shouted the man behind the counter. Zizzi speed hovered over the square between the shop and the cathedral. Fortunately, it was dark and the Earthlings couldn't see how he was moving so fast. The Gareth and several others were following him, though.

Only the Gareth saw him jump up. As Zizzi landed on the West Face of the cathedral, next to his Scout, the battery on the suit finally gave up altogether. He now sat there in his Zogoid form.

"Can you see him?" called the Mum. The Gareth turned to face her.

"I… er…" he started.

Zizzi hurried into the Scout and set her off through the Earth's atmosphere. He would have to do two orbits to get her up to power. He flicked on the Ranger's screen and zoomed on to the cathedral. The Gareth and the Mum were talking to a man in a dark navy uniform.

"He just seemed to jump up," said the Gareth. "But when I looked up there was nothing but a couple of those funny statues. One was about six times as big as the other."

The man in uniform sighed and shut his note book. He looked up.

"Are you on something, Sonny?" he said. "There are no gargoyles on the West Face."

The main screen of the Scout's communication system crackled on. It was the Mentor. Zizzi had been dreading this.

"Well that didn't go too well, did it? You know you will lose your Scout licence if you reveal yourself three times without permission from Explorer Corps. You must be more careful, Zizzi."

Zizzi hung his head.

"Well, anyway, cheer up. Did you find out any more about the gargoyles?"

"Well, there aren't any on the West Face of Winchester Cathedral."

"Hm. Was that worth the risk?"

"And I have got a book."

"You stole a book, you mean."

"Mmm. Yes."

"Well, we'll have to find a way to compensate."

"Actually, I was thinking."

"Yes?"

"Maybe gargoyles aren't so interesting. I'd like to find out more about the Gareth. And perhaps about that baby."

57

"Well, perhaps. We'll discuss it when you get back to Zogo. Peace to Zogoids."

"Peace to Zogoids."

Zizzi was now leaving the Earth's orbit. He took one last look at the planet. It looked like a giant marble, all blue and white swirls. It would be good to return to Zogo, where life was easy and pleasant and much more modern than on Earth. But he would be back! Oh yes, he would be back!

The Lady Rose

"We won't be too long. We should be back before it's dark."

"And don't let any strangers in. Oh, I wish you'd come with us. I don't like leaving you on your own."

"I'll be all right, Mum."

"She will. Nobody'll be able to get in anyway. The bank's too steep."

Kerry wished they would just get going. She'd not had any privacy to talk to Alex since they'd come on this stupid holiday and she was dying to call him without her parents hearing. "Just go. I'm fourteen now. I can look after myself."

At last she heard the dinghy rowing away from the houseboat. She took out her phone and found Alex's number.

"So you haven't forgotten me, then," he said when he answered. "I thought you must be having so much fun with your mum and dad going up and down the Broads on the Lady Rose."

"Ha! Ha! Never been so bored in my life!"

"Ooh. I wish you was here so that I could snog you."

Me too, thought Kerry. "I wish you was here and all. I'm all alone on the boat. There's two lovely cosy cabins."

"Don't say that. That's just too frustrating."

"What you been doing anyway?"

"Oh you know. Not much."

But she bet he had. They'd have all gone off to McDonald's or the cinema. And Lucy would have been there. She didn't trust Lucy. Lucy fancied Alex and made no secret of it.

Her phone pipped twice. Damn. It had lost the signal. So much for having a nice romantic talk with Alex then.

Still, it was good having some time to herself. She did her nails and washed her hair. She listened to her iPod for a bit, until the battery ran flat. She plugged it in to recharge and then she made herself a coffee. She flicked though the magazines she'd brought with her.

She tried her phone again. No signal.

She was getting hungry. Hopefully her parents would also bring some food with them when they came back with someone to look at the boat.

She went to her cabin and picked up her book. She couldn't settle to read it though. She even considered doing some of the homework she'd brought with her. But no, that would be desperate. She wasn't quite that bored.

She'd been sitting still for quite a long time and was beginning to get cold. Perhaps she could go to sleep for a bit. That might make the time go quicker. She went back to her cabin and snuggled down under the duvet. She was soon warm and she drifted into a gentle doze. She didn't think she actually slept. Something must have happened though. Her legs suddenly jerked and she sat upright in bed. It was dark now. But there was a red glow coming from the main deck.

"Hi, Mum, Dad," she called. Had they got back and were they doing something to the boat?

There was no answer.

She flicked the light switch. Nothing happened. Well, they had warned her about that. They'd said the power wouldn't last very long. But why weren't they back yet? What was the time? She picked up her phone. Darn! The battery had gone now. Oh, great. Even if she could get her signal back they wouldn't be able to let her know anything.

She rummaged in her drawer for her torch and flicked it on, so that she could see her wristwatch. Blimey! It was half past eight. Where were they?

So what was that red light, anyway?

She edged her way on to the main deck. The light was in fact bright enough for her to be able to see where she was going. It cast a really strange glow over the small area. She could see now that it was coming from a bulb on the dashboard. She switched her torch on so that she could read the writing next to the bulb. "Pump-out required." What the heck did that mean? Then she remembered half-heartedly watching the man at the boatyard giving her dad instructions about looking after the houseboat. "If that light comes on," he'd said. "You'll have to get her to the nearest service depot and have the septic tank pumped out. Don't let anybody go to the lavatory until it's done."

Oh gross! She wouldn't even be allowed to go for a pee now. She was convinced she could smell raw sewage. This really sucked. Where the hell were they?

Could something have happened to them? It was getting really worrying now. She shivered and her tummy rumbled.

There were a few biscuits she thought, in the kitchen cupboard. She felt for the door and found the biscuits and a half-full box of cereal. That would keep her going a bit at least. Of course, she'd used up the last of the milk in her coffee.

She felt her way back to her cabin and sat munching the biscuits and the cereal with the duvet wrapped round her. When she'd had enough, she snuggled back down into bed.

It was annoying, this? Where the heck were they? Perhaps they couldn't get back up the river with help because of the tide. Perhaps they couldn't get under the bridges. Yes, that would be it. They'd be back in the morning, she guessed. Anyway, once it was light she might be able to get help. She might even be able to get off the boat and walk across the fields. The steep bank would be a bit of a challenge but she was sure she'd manage it if she could see what she was doing. Best get some sleep now. Yes, that would be the best idea. It got light early enough these days. Sleeping would make the morning come more quickly.

When she woke with a start later she had the sense that a couple of hours had gone by. And she needed a pee. Did she dare use the loo, though?

The sickly smell of sewage warned that she shouldn't. Best use a bucket and throw it overboard. Gross. Bloody parents. Bugger them for bringing her on this holiday in the first place, and for leaving her on her own and for letting the septic tank get full.

She reached out for her torch. She couldn't find it. Perhaps she'd knocked it off the bedside table. She knelt down on the floor and felt for it. It was no good. It just wasn't there. She didn't fancy trying to find the bucket in the dark. Could she manage to go over the side of the boat? What if she fell in? She'd have to do something, though. She'd wet herself if she didn't go soon. Oh why couldn't she have been born a bloke? They had it easier.

She fumbled her way on to the outer deck. There was a little bit of moonlight and her eyes soon adjusted enough for her to be able to see what she was doing. It was cool out there, despite it being the middle of August. She managed to make her way over to the side that was away from the bank. She undid her trousers and pulled them and her pants down. She took her jumper off and tied it round her waist and then tied each arm though one of the rings on the side of the boat. She just managed to position her bottom so that it was over the side of the boat. Then for some reason, she couldn't pee.

"Come on, come on," she muttered to herself. She was dying to go and yet she couldn't. It did come, eventually and then she couldn't stop. It must have been one of the most unsuccessful wees she'd ever had. Because she wasn't far enough over the side of the boat not much of it went into the water but ran down her legs and then into her trousers. It was a relief, though all the same and she guessed that in the grander scheme of things it didn't matter that much.

She fumbled her way back to her cabin, stripped her trousers and pants off and managed to find some clean ones. She was shivering now. She guessed it was partly because she was scared. It wasn't really all that cold.

She still didn't want to get undressed and get into bed properly. She thought she'd better be ready for anything. She lay on the bed and pulled the duvet over her. She couldn't sleep, though. Perhaps she should change her mind about getting undressed? If she got into bed properly maybe she would sleep? She dismissed that thought. She knew she'd got to be prepared for all eventualities though she wasn't quite sure what she was expecting.

Surely it must get light soon? The days were still pretty long. The night couldn't last forever, could it?

The she heard the scrabbling noise. What could that be? Rats, perhaps? They couldn't have got into the toilet tank, could they? Surely it was all sealed in? She held her breath. The noise stopped. What, so it had been her own chest squeaking as she breathed? Maybe. She had to breathe again eventually.

Then she heard something else. A sort of creaking. Was the tide changing? Would she need to go out and adjust the ropes? Surely she it had been low tide when they moored here? At least that would mean that worse the boat would float away from the bank a little. That wasn't disastrous. If need be tomorrow she could swim over to the other bank. She tried to look out of the small cabin window. She couldn't see a thing. It was as black as ever out there. She pressed her ear against the class. Yes, she could hear water running. The tide was surely changing.

Suddenly the boat rocked. Her heart lurched. Had something bumped into it? She held her breath. It creaked above her. It sounded like a footstep. Then came another. Were they back?

She went to call out then just stopped herself in time. What if it wasn't them? It could be anybody. Could that sound of water running before have been a boat arriving? Surely not. It had been the wrong sort of sound. So, if there was someone out there, they'd come across the fields. Who would be out in the fields at this time of night?

Had she remembered to lock the main door? She thought she had. She moved as quietly as she could to her cabin door and slid the bolt across. She'd only done that once before, right at the beginning of the holiday. It had stuck and she'd had a real job to get it open. Her dad had told her not to lock it again. "It's not as if you've got anything to hide, have you? You don't lock yourself in at home, do you?" It would be a problem getting it open again tomorrow. But she would face that in daylight. For now, she just needed to keep whoever was up there out.

It had gone quiet above her. Had she imagined it? Could it have perhaps been some sort of animal? She held her breath again and listened carefully.

Then the footsteps began again. They were definitely human. She heard him rattle the door. Well, at least that proved that she'd locked it. That was something. The footsteps went back again. She heard him jump from the boat and land on the bank. So, it was possible to get on to the bank. Then nothing.

She lay still for what she thought was about ten minutes. Tentatively then she stretched over towards the small window and raised the small blind. A hideous face was looking in. A mouth opened into a wide grin and she could see some rotten teeth and gaps where other teeth ought to have been.

She let the blind drop and flung herself back down on the bed. This was a nightmare. This must be a nightmare and she would wake up any moment now. Please let it be a nightmare.

She lay shivering on her bed for another ten minutes. Then she lifted the blind again. No one there. What should she do?

She decided she was going to get away. If she went off across the fields she'd get to civilisation eventually. She found a warm jumper and pulled it on. She still couldn't find the torch. But perhaps it would be lighter outside and her eyes would get used to it.

She managed to undo the bolt on her cabin door without any trouble. Perhaps she'd loosened it the first time or perhaps she'd got stronger because she was scared. Either way, she was out in seconds and could actually now see quite well to find her way to the main door. The clouds had cleared completely now and the moon was shining brightly. She opened the door and stepped onto the outer deck.

He was standing there. He was holding a drill.

"Get out of my way, you pervert!" she cried as she pushed past him.

The man lost his footing and fell neatly into the water.

"I hope you drown," she muttered. She jumped for the bank. She landed fine but her left foot turned as it hit the ground, making her slip and hit her head on the mooring post. Stars twirled above her head and she had a pleasant warm feeling as she felt herself slip into the water, feet first.

She was going to die. She was sure of it. She tried to imagine what it would be like at her funeral and wondered whether Alex would cry.

When she came to she was back in her bed inside her cabin. She was in her pyjamas. Light was streaming in thought the window.

Had she dreamt it all? Her head did hurt, though. And she could hear someone knocking on the cabin door.

"Police!" cried a female voice. "May we come in?"

"I don't believe you," said Kerry. "Go away."

"Well, if we'd wanted to hurt you we would have come in by now. Look out of your window. And here's my ID card."

Kerry raised the blind again. Sure enough she could see a policeman standing on the bank. He waved and smiled.

She pulled herself out of bed and picked up the card that the police officer had pushed under the door. It looked genuine enough but you could never be too sure, could you?

"You might be pretending to be police officers. How do I know you're real?"

"You'll just have to believe us, Kerry, my love. We've come to tell you about your parents. There's been an accident. But don't worry. They're going to be all right."

She opened the door. The police woman smiled at her.

"There was a man here. I pushed him in the water." Kerry thought she was going to be sick. What if she'd killed him?

"We know. He came and told us this morning. In fact, if it hadn't have been for him we wouldn't have found your boat so quickly. He was able to tell us exactly where you were moored."

"That's right, love. Tom Jenkins. He's a bit simple, but harmless enough. He didn't do anything to you, did he?"

66

Kerry shook her head.

"Good."

"So, would you like to get some clothes on and we'll take you to your parents." The policewoman rubbed her arm and smiled.

The sick feeling went away. She felt quite relaxed as she had a quick wash in cold water and then got dressed. Until she noticed the two large bruises on her thighs and remembered she had no idea how she had got out of the water and into bed.

Chocolate

Billy Elkins pressed the send button. He watched as 500 messages made their way to members of the Ambosso Advertising Group and thought it just a little ironic that the people receiving the message were seen as clients and that indeed the company he worked for was called an advertising company. Since the Bank Dissolution Act there had been no actual competition and no need to advertise, really, except by the people who needed work doing. Which reminded him he must find someone to paint his bathroom ceiling. He would add that to Monday's list. He suspected there would be a long wait.

Still, that was him done for the week. Since he was obliged to work until he was sixty-eight, he was at least grateful that the demands of Ambosso were not too onerous, that he got to work in a pleasant office and that even as a bachelor, he was allowed a two-bedroomed apartment.

"Coming for a drink?" asked Ronnie Parkinson, his colleague at the next desk. Ronnie was the same age as him but had been with Ambosso two years longer and seemed to know so much more about everything.

Why not? It would give him a bit of the old Friday night feeling. It wasn't the same, now, though, when you didn't have to stop to think about whether you had enough money left to buy beer and you only had to worry about whether the pub actually had any. Still, chances were, if they didn't have beer, they'd have something.

Minutes later, the two men were making their way out of the sleek modern offices that housed Ambosso and weaving their way between other modern sky-scrapers.

The Tap and Bucket was like an echo from the old days. Dwarfed by the buildings either side it looked totally out of place. However, the minute Billy stepped through the door he could forget the busy city. It smelt like a pub, though he still missed the smoky atmosphere from before the smoking ban.

"Pint of Amber?" Ronnie asked him.

Billy nodded.

Ronnie winked at the barman. "I'm in the know," he said, turning to Billy. "They had a delivery this morning."

"I'm afraid we're limiting you to two pints each," the barman said.

Ronnie shrugged. "Well, it's pretty strong," he said. "We should be all right."

They settled themselves in a corner.

"Good vantage point here," said Ronnie. "We should get a good view of everybody who comes in."

The Amber was good. A fine old real ale. Creamy. Rich. Billy enjoyed feeling the foam crackling in his moustache. It slid down his throat so easily. He was just beginning to get that longed-for Friday night feeling. And yes, he had a couple of days of freedom before he was due in the office again. He'd got his name down for fishing and a cinema visit but hadn't had any confirmation yet so he guessed he wouldn't be doing that this weekend. At least the Box, the dataserve and the cycle path were always available though he was also on the list for a new bike.

Certainly, they could still make really good real ale.

"Told you this was a good spot," said Ronnie nodding towards the door.

It was Janita Smith and Alex Green from Accounts. Yes they still had accounts but they weren't anything to do with money any more. It was just as well. Those two didn't have a clue about numbers.

Yes, numbers. And two and two made four. There were two of them and two girls. He'd had a bit of a thing about

Janita for a long time. Alex wasn't bad either. Could be fun.

"Over here, ladies," Ronnie called.

The girls finished getting their drinks and ambled over to where Billy and Ronnie were sitting.

"Nice to see you here," said Janita. She was looking straight at Ronnie and ignoring him completely.

It was soon evident to Billy that he had no chance with Janita. She and Ronnie were flirting outrageously. He tried to make conversation with Alex but it was hard going. Perhaps another drink would help. "I'm going to get me another pint," he said. "Can I get you anything while I'm there?"

Alex looked at her watch. "Better not," she said. "Tim will be here in a few minutes."

Ah. Tim. Boyfriend he supposed.

He got his second pint. He had to wait about twenty minutes. When he got back to the table, Alex was just disappearing through the door with a guy Billy assumed must be Tim. Ronnie and Janita were pulling on their coats.

"We're going to Berties," said Ronnie. "Janita's got a couple of tickets. Sorry mate. Enjoy your pint. See you Monday."

It was only just light when Billy woke up on Saturday morning. "Darn!" he muttered as he looked at the alarm clock. It was actually earlier than the time he had to get up in the week. But he was wide awake. May as well get up, then.

He went to make coffee and discovered there was only about enough for one more breakfast. He quickly checked the dataserve. That was something at least. He was due a food allowance and he could pick it up at the local supermarket this morning. Good, then, that he was up early. Get that out of the way and have the rest of the day to himself.

As soon as he raised the shutters, however, his slightly better mood darkened again. The sky was grey and it was pouring with rain. The journey to the supermarket would be a trial. No way would he be going out on his bike today. Even a walk seemed out of the question.

He was completely soaked by the time he arrived. The queues at the checkout and the taxi rank were enormous. By the time he got home again it was almost lunchtime. And it was still raining. Pouring, in fact.

That left him with the dataserve and the Box. The Box had been dismal last night. No wonder with that and the Amber, he'd fallen asleep early which probably explained why he'd also woken up so early. Nothing but greyness then. At least when he used to worry about money all the time, he'd get quite a high when his bank account was in credit.

He noticed he had a phone message waiting and then realised that he'd also missed a call on his mobile. Ronnie. Well, better see what the old rogue wanted. That at least might be interesting. He pressed the speed dial for Ronnie.

"Hiya, Billy, me old mate," said Ronnie. "Sorry about last night. But you ain't having a lot of luck with the ladies, are you?"

"No, I suppose I'm not really," said Billy. That was an understatement if ever there was one.

"Well, I think we should do something about that, don't you?" said Ronnie.

"I suppose," said Billy. Why on earth did he think he could do it? You either had it or you didn't. Ronnie did. He didn't. Just a fact of life, he guessed.

"Can I come round?" asked Ronnie.

"I suppose," said Billy. Why not? Ronnie was okay. He spent every working day with him and he was actually good company. It was only when girls were involved that he was a bit unpredictable. So why not?

"Okey, dokey," said Ronnie. "See you in ten."

Just fifteen minutes later the doorbell rang. Seconds after that, Billy was opening the door to his apartment. He offered Ronnie a coffee.

"You've got to offer the ladies something that other blokes don't have," said Ronnie, as he sipped his drink.

"But I don't have even what you've got," said Billy. "You're lucky. You're a born charmer."

"Ah, nuts," said Ronnie. "I couldn't keep that up forever. Too much like hard work." He put his coffee cup down and put his hand into his pocket. "This is what they follow me for," he said.

He was holding a large bar of milk chocolate. "They stay with me because I have access to a never-ending supply of this stuff," he said.

"What?" said Billy. Chocolate was strictly rationed. There was only a certain amount in the food allowance and then only if you didn't have cakes or biscuits or other sweet things.

"Wouldn't you like to know?" said Ronnie. "But you know what, because you're such a mate I'm going to show you. Have you got one of your old bank cards still?"

"Why?" said Billy.

"Well, do you have one or not?" said Ronnie.

"Yes," said Billy. Where was this going? Bank cards were no use at all these days. Billy wasn't even sure why he'd kept his.

"Well, come on then," said Ronnie. "Go get it, quick."

Five minutes later they were walking towards what used to be the high street, now deserted. Most of the old shops were boarded up. Since the riots just before the banks were shut down most people preferred to shop online.

"Best not to let anybody see you," said Ronnie. "We don't want too many people knowing the secret."

Ronnie looked over his shoulder. Billy turned too and noticed they were completely alone.

"Okay," said Ronnie. He walked over to one of the ATMs that belonged to what used to be Billy's bank.

"Stick the card in," said Ronnie.

Billy did as he was told and the panel sprang into life and asked for his pin. He typed it in. Next, instead of asking whether he wanted cash with or without a receipt or a statement, though it did mention pin services, it asked him whether he wanted a 100 gram block, a 200 gram block, an individual snack, a small selection or other.

"The 200 gram blocks are the best here, mate," said Ronnie.

The ATM whirred and clicked and from a much bigger opening than the one that used to deliver bank notes, out popped a large bar of chocolate wrapped in purple and silver.

"How?" said Billy. "And how did you know?"

"Used to work at Crumblies Bank before the Act," said Ronnie. "Knew this was coming. But keep quiet about it. Don't whatever you do tell any of the ladies where you get the goods from"

When Billy called for Janita that evening he was delighted that she had dressed up for him.

"Thank you so much," she crooned as he handed her the 200 gram bar. She kissed him lightly on the cheek and stowed her bounty away in the fridge. "Let's get going, shall we?"

She'd got tickets for Berties again.

Billy was glad that Ronnie had suggested he should give her a ring and that he should mention the purple and silver package. As they stepped out on to the wet pavement he patted his inside jacket pocket to make sure that his bank card was safely there. He would have to start using it regularly again.

Her Angel Eyes

It's the doll that convinces me. The doll that Georg gave her. A bit of a mean thing and now even more battered. Made of ivory. It belonged to his mother and her mother before her. And now here it is a bit dirty and crumpled but still intact.

She loved that doll. She never had much, poor kid. And never a doll. The Goldbergs didn't understand little girls that much. They didn't have a lot of time. She had six brothers. They understood boys better. Besides, it was never easy for people like the Goldbergs. Not even here. A lot of them have always lived here. They were decent people. You know exactly what I mean.

Our Gisela was so generous. She always liked playing with Emi. And she didn't mind a bit that her daddy had given her friend this family heirloom. But anyway, Gisela had plenty of other toys. It was easier for us. We weren't like the Goldbergs.

I used to invite Frau Goldberg in for coffee sometimes. The poor woman was run off her feet looking after seven men. Yes, the boys were big and hefty, even Eli, the youngest. He was just eleven. She was so thin. Any energy she got from what she did eat went straight into looking after her family. The only bit she got for herself was if I found a scrap of cake to go with our coffee.

"We've got to be careful," Georg used to say. "Some will say we're associating with the state enemy."

But I didn't get that at all. The Goldbergs were just people in my eyes. And anyway, who was going to tell? There were more of them than of us. That is, more of them were taken away that night than were left here afterwards.

You know, that poor child was just seven years old the night they came for them. It was a warm evening. Everyone

75

had their doors and windows open. There was a full moon too. There was a lot of light. Lots of people were outside already. We saw exactly what happened.

We didn't have any warning, though. They arrived so suddenly. One minute everyone was just going about their normal business. The next, the trucks were here and those brutal men in their grey uniforms. They had dogs as well. It only took ten minutes in the end. Until they had gone with all of the families.

It's not as if anybody would have given them away. They were our friends. All of them. Not just the Goldbergs. In a small place like this everybody knows each other and everybody looks after each other. The authorities knew exactly who lived here anyway. They knew exactly who they were looking for. It was just a matter of time before it happened, I suppose.

The men in uniform started yelling "Scum, out!" They pushed people on to the trucks. Their dogs were snarling and nipping at their ankles.

There were just one or two doors that were shut. The officers hammered on those and if they weren't opened straight away, they broke them down. In most cases the doors had been shut because nobody was home. So, they'd broken the doors for nothing. One of them kept firing his gun in the air. I've never heard a gun so close before. It was terrifying.

It was awful watching the Goldbergs being taken away. They were my friends and they looked so helpless. Herr Goldberg was a strong man and so were the boys. But they couldn't do anything. I thought Frau Goldberg was going to faint.

Emi was just standing there. My husband gathered her and Gisela up and ran into the house with them. He was acting as if both girls were our daughters and he didn't want

76

them to see that horrible scene. Which father would?

Then he ran with Emi into the back garden. He helped her over the wall. "Run as fast as you can," he said. "I'll come and find you tomorrow. Once the men have gone."

We're lucky that our house backs on to the forest. Off she scampered, eyes round and scared-looking. She was clutching the doll. Wouldn't let it go.

They'd seen her run from the house. Seconds later they came looking for her.

"Where did that girl go?" asked one of the soldiers.

I didn't say anything. I was still frozen.

"She jumped over the garden wall back into the house," said Georg.

Of course they went back and ruined another good door. And they took some of the Goldberg's possessions. I saw them stuffing some of Frau Goldberg's nice china into the cab of one of the trucks.

Georg went back and looked for her as soon as the trucks had gone. And then the next day as soon as it was light. Several more times that day. Then we heard that the soldiers had come back and rounded up all of the ones who had escaped into the forest. We actually heard them shooting people. We didn't know then that the Goldbergs had never registered Emi's birth.

They didn't stop to look that night. So Emi wasn't the only one to get away. They came back for the others the next day. They knew everybody was scared and that we wouldn't help or hide any of the people they were after.

Our little one, Gisela, was more frightened than Emi had been, I think. She was jumpy for days afterwards. The slightest sound and she would cling to my legs like a toddler and bury her head in my lap.

We never really gave up. We hoped for a while that we might find Emi despite what they'd said. And then even when we believed that she had been shot we still looked for traces of her in the forest. But there was nothing. Nothing at all.

Not until we heard about the Wild Woman. Oh, there'd always been stories about the Wild Woman living in the forest. When I was young girl my mother used to tell me about her. Of course, when I got older I realised that it was just a story she made up to stop us straying too far. The forest is so untamed and dense round here you could get lost for days. As is perfectly clear now. In fact it's evident you can get lost for years.

They called the young woman they found last week the Wild Woman because she looks unkempt, uncared for. Because she ran like a wild animal when they tried to help her. And because she won't speak.

We all went out to watch when they took her from the police station to the hospital. I know she's not a woman. She's barely more than a girl. The same age as my Gisela. And look at the state of her. Compared with my daughter who at this very moment is sitting comfortably in a classroom studying for her Abitur.

She was holding the doll.

Wild yes, she's wild. Woman no. She's a girl.

The forest is rich. It would be possible to live there for seven years. You can forage. There are animals to kill. She was wearing animal skins. Not proper clothes. Everybody could see that. And there are berries to eat. There's even water to drink.

Yes, I'm absolutely convinced that this is Emi and she wouldn't have dropped the doll. If she needed both hands free, she'd have hidden it somewhere safe. Besides, there was something about the way she was carrying it. Holding it to her like you would a baby.

Anyway, it's got a chip on the back of its head. I

remember our Leo – Gisela's older brother – banging it on the fender when the three of them got into a fight over something really silly. If I can see it close to I'll be able to tell.

They say she doesn't talk. She used to be a right little chatterbox. But think about it. She had to watch her family being taken away. Then she heard some of her friends being shot. On top of all of that, she's been on her own for seven years. And then the way they found her last week. They say she's pregnant. How did that happen? How would she have understood what was happening to her? Would anybody want to talk after all of that?

They're letting me see her close to, now. I'm really nervous. Just suppose it isn't her after all? Or she doesn't want to see me? Or she gets upset?

"You can come in, now, Frau Kellermann," the woman says. She's a bit snooty. Talks through her nose. "We can't promise anything. But yes, she could do with some friends right now. Try not to get too attached, though. And don't let her get too dependent on you. Just in case."

I open the door to the side ward. The girl is lying with her back to me. She turns to face me. I gasp. She looks so much like a younger version of Frau Goldberg.

She just stares blankly at me.

I notice her rounded belly. Was it rape then?

They've put the doll on the bedside cabinet. I reach out and pick it up.

She whimpers and stretches out her arms.

I have to check it first, though. Yes, the dent is there. It is definitely Emi's doll.

I hold it to her. Her face lights up and I hand it to her. A faint smile appears on her lips.

Then she's holding it, rocking it like a real baby. Dear God, I hope when that baby's born she'll know to love it

79

and hold it like that. Goodness knows she's had enough practice with the doll.

Then she looks up and I see her dark brown eyes.

Her angel eyes.

Unmistakably Emi.

Big Blue

"I want to move into this area, and this is where people like you come in – because artists and writers aren't constrained by the scientific processes. You can speculate, imagine yourself in the world of the whale. And then open-minded scientists, by looking at what artists produce, may make hypotheses that will lead us onto paths that will begin to crack these great mysteries." Philip Hoare

http://www.theguardian.com/science/2011/jan/30/ whales-philip-hoare-hal-whitehead
Accessed 08/08/2014

The scientists can give us the facts and without those facts I couldn't write this story let alone make it in any way authentic. I choose however to write the heart of the story.

He glides through the deep blue water. He maintains a pace of about five miles an hour. This is the speed he likes. It isn't hurried. Every so often he comes to the surface to breathe, pushing out a huge jet of water. Then back down in to the silky wetness that is his home.

The cold doesn't bother him. It never has. It's what he knows. He notices it though. He feels as well the sun that warms him as he lingers a short while on the surface.

Then down to the depths, mouth open, then closed and pushing out the water, leaving the krill behind. His belly feels empty and will take a while to fill yet. Still he punctuates his time in the depths with trips up to the surface. Pull in, push out, pull in, push out then push up and push out again. Now dive down into the cold depths. Until, at last, he is satisfied and can linger for longer just below the surface.

The sun invites him to play. He jumps high out of the water and anyone watching must assume he is full of joy. Yes, a true jump for joy, a leap of faith, as his tail flicks off water. Three times he repeats this, twirling his whole body round the final time, slapping the surface hard as he lands. His skin now feels fresh and parasite-free.

He is fed. He is clean. He has exercised. Sleepy and relaxed he floats like a log with the water just covering him.

He dozes but something comes through the deep, penetrates his dreams and now he is alert. "Wohm, wohm, wohm." With a higher-pitched echo. He recognises at once the call of the calf and its mother. He turns himself to be in a vertical position, pushes his head out of the water and looks around but sees nothing.

"Wohm, wohm, wohm," he hears again. He puts his head back under the water and can feel the direction of the call.

Now he is fully alert and begins to swim towards the sound with all of his strength. He accelerates up to and beyond his earlier five miles an hour. Soon he is charging along at twenty, anxious to meet them.

A squeaker-whistler joins him. Normally he wouldn't mind. They're company of a sort and often help to pick out a sensible route through the waves. This one, though, is irritating. She squeaks at him constantly, jabs at his head and seems to want to push him away. She's no match for him of course. One flick and he could crush her but some instinct stops him from doing that. Then every so often she lets out one of her piercing whistles. It sounds like a warning. If only he could understand her language.

She will not let him alone.

She nudges him again with her nose. He turns slightly.

A shadow falls across the water. Something is not right. His mate's call is nearer but not so near for this to be her.

82

What other animal could be so big to cast such a shadow?

Now the squeaker-whistler is actually nipping his side, forcing him to turn. Now she is jabbering away even more ferociously. He can no longer hear his mate easily.

Almost too late he recognises what causes the shadow. It is the machine that humans use because they're not so good at swimming. He tries to turn away from it but it's a struggle. He hears the human voices. They are just as frenetic as the squeaker-whistler. They seem to have as much difficult turning as he does. The machine's roar drowns out his mate's call altogether.

Somehow they manage to avoid each other. There is the smallest gap between them and the squeaker would have been crushed if she had not jumped so expertly out of the way. He'd encountered one of these machines before and had not been so lucky with no squeaker to help. The machine had turned over that time, spilling its human riders into the ocean and he'd grazed his side badly. The scar still throbbed sometimes in the cold depths.

His heart races. He can still hear them coming towards them. They will run into the machine, too, if he doesn't warn them. He lifts his great tail and slaps it down on to the surface of the water. Several times rapidly. He utters a warning, to them and others of his kind.

The squeaker whistles. She's probably sending a message as well to her kind. Just as urgently by the sounds of it.

The mother and calf return his call. They understand, it seems. They are heading north. The human machine is travelling now towards the south. The danger is over. For the moment at least. He sends a confirmation message.

The squeaker jumps over his nose and dives beneath him. She squeaks quietly then nudges him gently. He needs to surface and as he does she jumps again, landing on his nose. He dives again and she swims in front to him. She seems to sense when he is going to surface and three times comes up with him, lying on his nose. He tosses her gently into the air. She swims round him and under him and then jumps across him. He lines himself up a little beyond where she lands.

They travel along swiftly now but not urgently.

She gives him one more nudge and then turns west, squeaking and whistling as she goes.

Big Blue turns a little more to the north. A mother and child are waiting for him there. He relishes the sun each time he surfaces. He will be there soon. He accelerates up to twenty miles an hour again.

Access Denied

You could smell them, the people who lived in the underpass. The stench hit you before you were even within 200 yards of them. There must be about fifty there now. More arrived every day. Bob was used to it now, though. This was, anyway, the only route into town now that he couldn't renew his transport chip.

It got worse the nearer he got to them. Even he, hardened as he was, had to hold his breath and rush through them. He knew never to indulge in eye contact. Keep looking at the ground. That was the trick. This was fine until he tripped over what he had assumed was someone's bag. The outer cover fell away, revealing the corpse of a new-born baby. He couldn't help but look into the eyes of the mother.

"Sorry," he mumbled.

Two dark eyes looked into his. *Why?* She blinked and nodded slightly. *You too?*

Bob shuddered inside and hurried on.

The still-functioning ATM was on the corner of Park Road and the Avenue. There had been a bank there once but it was a smart Italian restaurant now. Even today it was packed with diners in casual smart. It was all still working for some, then. At least they'd left the cash machine there. There were fewer and fewer of them these days.

There was no queue. Bob took out his debit card and slid it into the slot.

Processing your details flashed on to the screen. *Enter your pin.*

Bob tapped the day and month of his first girlfriend's birthday on to the key pad. The machine clicked and whirred for several seconds.

Access Denied.

This was madness. There was at least 400 New Pounds in his account. Even if it wouldn't go very far it would do something. Why couldn't he get at it? Annoying that he would now have to contact the bank and sort that out. Hours then of piped music, robotic voices and pressing keys.

He still had his Union Credit card. He would have to use that. Even though he begrudged the 10% service charge. Even though it would mean that his rental payment wouldn't clear.

He took out the sky-blue card with the silver lettering and slid it into the slot. The machine snatched it.

Enter your pin.

He typed in the first four numbers of the registration plate of the car he'd been given on his eighteenth birthday.

The machine whirred and clicked for even longer this time until finally the screen lit up. *Access denied.*

What now? He still had credit on that card too. The Alliance must have censored him. This must mean he was under investigation. There was nothing he could do now except hope that Suzie had managed to find something.

He slid his wallet back into his pocket. He would just have to walk back home.

It was uphill all the way back. He was out of breath even before he got to the underpass. He paused before he entered, trying to get his breath back so that he could hold it before he went through. It didn't work. The smell was overpowering. He wondered how they managed to live with it.

Oddly, he found himself dawdling, looking for the woman with the dead baby but there was no sign of her. He was worried about her. Why though? She was a complete stranger. What was she to him? He'd never be like one of them. Sure, it was tough now, but they'd get through it. It had happened before and they'd come good in the end. They could do it again.

Out of the underpass he continued to go slowly up the hill. Would Susie be home? Would she have something sorted? He wanted to hurry and find out but he couldn't will his feet to go any faster. Was he scared of what might be waiting for him?

At last he arrived at Beech Tree View. The sun had just come out from behind the clouds. The gardens looked as trim as ever. Life was holding on against the Alliance, then. Or so some folk were pretending. Most folk actually. Even his own lawn was impeccable and the roses had been expertly pruned and fed. You just had to keep up appearances.

He walked up the path and put his hand on the scanner. The door swung open and he knew at once that there was something wrong.

It was the coldness that hit him first. What, had the heating stopped working? Or worse, had the Alliance Bank failed to make this month's payment and they'd been cut off? Had he done something wrong? He tried to think what he might have done to annoy them.

"Susie?" he called.

No answer.

He couldn't hear her in the kitchen. Perhaps she was upstairs.

He made his way up to their bedroom. "Susie?"

He gasped as he opened the door. The bedding had been folded neatly and piled up on the bed. Susie's wardrobe was open and empty. What had happened?

The live-messenger was blinking, showing there was a recording. "Play!" he whispered.

Susie's face came on to the screen. "It's over, Rob. They came this afternoon. They said they had a place for me and Vicky at Alliance Headquarters. There's nothing for you, Rob. I'm sorry."

He replayed the recording. Was that a slight catch in her voice? Did that mean she still cared? What about Vicky? Why hadn't she put Vicky on?

He looked around the room. His things were still there, and the live-messenger. And downstairs all the furniture was there and all of the electric goods, he thought. He'd go and check in a minute. There was a little, hope, then.

He walked slowly downstairs. He wondered how long it would be before the landlord put in an appearance. Would he be able to reason with him – or was it her? All he ever knew was that it was M McTavers. He doubted it was going to be possible. If Susie and Vicky were already on their way to Alliance HQ that meant all hope was gone. Once you were taken over by the Alliance that was it.

As soon as he opened the lounge door the live-messenger there started to blink. Rob sighed. "Play." He half hoped the machine would not hear him properly.

The name M McTavers flashed across the screen. She seemed very young and much too glamorous to be a landlord. Shiny ginger hair came down to her shoulders. Her lips were painted bright red. Her eyes looked like ice. "Mr Reynolds, we're sending in the bailiffs to seize goods at least up to the value of the unpaid rent. Do not attempt to leave until our agents have indicated which personal effects you may remove from the property. If you should choose to do so we shall not hesitate to trace the chip and issue an appropriate punishment. We can count on your compliance?"

Rob nodded.

"Thank you. The bailiffs will be with you shortly."

The live-messenger snapped off.

Rob almost wished they would hurry up. He wanted to get moving though he had no idea where he would go. It was getting very chilly in the house.

He didn't have to wait very long at all until an unmarked white van pulled up outside the house. Two well-built middle-aged men and a woman with a face as sour as vinegar got out. The woman was frowning and holding a clipboard.

Rob hurried to open the door. He didn't want too many of the neighbours gawping. He realised that he was too late though. Already the Martins and the Johnsons were standing on their front doorsteps. Even the runny-nosed Evans twins had stopped playing to stare. Everybody knew what an unmarked white van meant.

The woman nodded as he let her in. She didn't get eye contact. She might have been nice-looking once, Rob thought, before she'd lost the habit of smiling.

"Start upstairs then?" said the taller of the two men.

"Yes, that would be right," said the woman, writing something down on her clipboard.

"You may as well go and get your stuff," said the shorter man. "Jim'll leave your room until last. It's one change of clothes and three changes of underwear. Two sets of sleepwear and a duvet, pillow and coverings. Something sentimental – you know pictures and stuff. No electrics. Personal toiletries. That's it. I'd go and get going, if I were you, and then sling your hook. You don't want to watch this." He turned and went into the kitchen.

"Some white goods here," Rob heard the man shout from the kitchen. "Two hundred New Pounds?"

Jim was as good as his mate's word. He'd started on Vicky's room first. Rob tried not to look as he came out with her little bed in pieces. He'd not thought to go in there earlier but now felt a bit relieved that all of the teddies and other toys had already gone. Presumably she'd been allowed to take them with her to the Alliance.

Rob went into his room and listlessly opened his

wardrobe. Best to take the better-wearing stuff he supposed. And his thickest jumper. He changed into a pair of jeans. They'd serve him better than the thin office-smart trousers he'd been wearing. He shoved his spares into his old sports bag that had been on top of the wardrobe for several months. Ever since he'd failed to pay his gym membership.

The woman bustled into the room. "Come along, Mr Reynolds. We've almost done. We don't want to have to wait for you." Her face softened slightly. "It's always the hardest, picking the sentimental thing. That your wife and little girl?" She pointed to a picture of Susie and Vicky on the wall.

Ron nodded.

"Well that will do very well. Mind you…" She tore at the back of the picture. "I'd take it out of the frame if I were you. Less to carry." She finished removing it and handed it to him. "Well then."

"Well then."

She nodded. "You may as well get going Mr Reynolds."

Rob turned to leave.

"Just one thing. You've made a slight profit. Thirty New Pounds. That might keep you going for a week or two."

She pulled a wad of notes out of her pocket and counted out three new ten pound notes.

The three of them were staring at him now. Jim cleared his throat. They were waiting for him to go. Was it one final sign of respect? That they wouldn't actually push him out but hang on until he was ready? Well, he'd better get it over with anyway.

They were still there, the Martins and the Johnsons and the scruffy Evans' kids. They stared at him as he walked out and down the road. The bedding was awkward to carry. He wished he'd tied it up with a belt. In the end, he slung the duvet round his shoulders and tucked the pillow under his arm. He heard one of the Evans' boys snigger and the adults start to whisper.

Best to ignore them, he thought. Best just to get on with it. Make it look as if he knew what he was doing. Well, at least he did know where he was going.

He hadn't got to the end of the road before the white van passed him. The horn tooted. He wished they hadn't done that. Even more people would know now.

He didn't notice the smell as he approached the underpass this time. He had other worries. The duvet draped around his shoulders was making him sweat. The sports bag had become quite heavy. He was glad to get there in the end even though that surprised him. This was to be home now.

It was dark in there but as his eyes got used to it he could make out that they were all staring at him. The stares were different, though, from those of the neighbours. He sensed curiosity, empathy not pity, and no superiority. No whispers or sniggers this time. He nodded at those with whom he got eye contact.

Someone tugged at his trousers. He looked down. It was her. The woman with the dead baby. She shuffled up to make room for him. She smiled. "You'll get used to it. We manage to make it bearable most of the time."

Rob folded up his duvet and made it into a seat. He sat down. "Your baby? What happened?"

"It didn't seem worth letting her live. I let her die."

Rob shuddered. Then, he figured, she had a point. He would get used to it, he supposed, but it would take some doing.

Extra Dimensions

"Well, it would be pretty impossible to get everybody to agree on a date," said Katie. "There's over forty of us now. Not even those of us here can agree."

Clive looked up at the twelve of them sitting round the four tables of the King's Arms. The beer was going flat. A waste of real ale. But it had only been bought as an excuse to sit at the tables for over an hour. He took a sip of the amber liquid. It tasted good but it was tepid now. Even getting the committee to agree on a date for the annual meal out was proving extremely tricky.

"Yes, but how many people have got iP 759s?" said Jake. "Most people now, right?"

"Yeah, but," said Dawson, "they creep most folk out."

Jake laughed. "Well they just need to get over that. It's not really a big deal at all. Look. It's just like saying you're going to the pub on Monday night. So, you leave the house at 7.30 Monday but get to the pub Tuesday evening. When you leave, you go back home late Monday evening. You've aged no more than normal. You might even look a bit young to the Tuesday night crowd. The pub is no longer just on the corner of Butly New Road and Donald Street. It's now also 26 January 2143."

"It's not natural, though," said Dawson.

"Neither is farming, email or even the basic mobi-com device," said Jake. "But could you imagine life without any of those?"

Several of the people round the tables mumbled.

"Okay, folks," said Jake. "I suggest we go for 26 January as most people can do that. Sorry, Clive, me old flower. You'll just have to use your iP."

The meeting was over. Half-finished beers were left on the table. Cars started. Clive hardly noticed the ride home.

He seemed to be there as soon as he'd left the pub. *I suppose it's the same sort of thing really,* he thought.

"You're not are you?" said Miranda. She was leaning over his shoulder as he tried to set the time regulator on his iP.

"Don't disturb me," he said. "It's complicated." It wasn't, actually, but he was a bit scared of getting it wrong. He didn't want to arrive in a strange place or at a funny time.

"Yes, but you hear about all of these people not coming back," said Miranda. "Or being a bit bonkers afterwards."

"That's rubbish," said Clive. He'd talked about it with Jake several times since the meeting in the pub. You had to return. The iP's failsafe whisked you back to your own timeline, even if you hadn't set it that way, once you'd used up the allowance. The allowance had been specifically designed so that people couldn't skitter about too much between different timelines. That way, there was less chance of any major temporal interference. And most people used it the way he intended to: just to juggle his diary a bit.

"It's not natural, though," said Miranda.

"We're paying enough for the darned thing," said Clive. "We may as well use it."

"Be careful, won't you?" said Miranda.

"It's only for the one night," said Clive. A blessed relief it would be, though, to get away from her constant nagging.

The meal with the archery club went very well in the end. At precisely 7.00 p.m. on the 25 of January he'd taken a shower then got ready. "I'll be going in a few minutes," he'd called to Miranda at 7.27. At precisely 7.30 his iP had buzzed and asked him to verify that he wanted to go to The Chinese Dragon, Old Street, Butly at 7.30, 26 January 2143.

He'd confirmed that that was correct. There's been a flash slightly less dramatic than when you download a book to an e-reader and there he was on the pavement outside The Chinese Dragon. He walked into the restaurant. The clock on the wall opposite said 7.31. Several members of the archery club were already there.

The evening passed pleasantly. All the important people from the club turned up. The food was superb. After each course, they'd change places so that everybody could mix with everybody else. He could have a drink or two as well as he hadn't got to give car instructions about how to get home. There were plenty of discussions about what they might do over the next twelve months. They were determined to get placed in the international competition next year.

Later people gradually began to leave. In a quiet moment, Clive gave the Return to Home Timeline command. There was another brief flash. He was back in his bedroom. The ceiling clock said it was 11.23. Miranda was already fast asleep. Good. He wouldn't be interrogated about how the evening had gone. *I could get used to this,* he thought.

Clive's head was buzzing louder than the alarm the next morning. Even before he was awake properly he had started doing some complex calculations. Maths was his forte after all. So, if the total allowance per month was 100 time tranches, he could actually use his allowance to avoid Miranda as much as possible. As a time tranche was the number of hours away multiplied by the number of days into the future or the past and the hours were calculated to the nearest $1/60^{th}$ and the days to the nearest $1/24^{th}$, if he only went a few minutes ahead or back each time, he could use almost 600 hours each month. Why hadn't anybody else thought of that?

Miranda and he had spent most of their married life trying to make their working shift patterns match. Now they were always at home together. It would be so easy to change with the iP. And what an irony. How much easier it would have been to keep together when they were young and in love. Now that they could fix it they didn't want that at all. Well, he didn't. He wasn't so sure about her but he presumed she was as irritated by him as he was by her.

Miranda was still in the bathroom. If he acted now, he could get away from her more or less permanently. He wouldn't even have to try to explain. Much better than a messy divorce or separation.

"Are you up, Clive?" he heard her call from the bathroom as he set the time regulator. "How was last night?"

Then, peace and quiet, as it was now 8.15 and she had already set off for work.

He soon got it down to a fine art. Whenever he should have been with Miranda he scooted forward a bit then came back to his own timeline for things like work, dentist appointments and archery club evenings.

They took to leaving each other notes on the dataserve messaging service. "We've been invited to see the Lawrences on Saturday," she said. "I presume you can make it and you'll pick up the wine. I'll do the flowers. Do you think we should take chocolates as well?"

He said: "Sorry. Had to get in early today. Old Pemberton wanted that report on his desk by ten. Needed to print it off and make copies."

Occasionally he would leave a more normal message. "Could you get my grey suit back from the cleaners, please?"

He took care not to overdo it though. He made sure they did meet up every now and then. But the best part was that for much of the time he could hover about a bit in the not too distant future and there would be no danger that she would suddenly walk in on him. He didn't go anywhere else. He just stayed in their home. It meant he could listen to his music in peace, watch the football, or even masturbate whilst watching a porn channel without her suddenly bursting in on him. Unless, of course, she tried a bit of time travelling herself. He somehow doubted that she would. She didn't like gadgets. And even if she did take it up, he doubted whether she would be able to pinpoint the exact futures he'd gone to; he always varied the times a little.

It was subtle at first and he didn't really quite believe that it was happening. It was their third visit to the Lawrences after he'd started using the iP 759's time travel function.

"You're looking well," said Geoff Lawrence, as he helped Miranda off with her coat and took the wine and flowers off her. "You look more beautiful every time I see you."

Geoff was ogling her, Clive realised. "That's my wife you're chatting up," he said, laughing. But as he looked at Miranda, he realised that Geoff was right. Her skin glowed, her eyes were bright and her hair was shining.

"Well, you take good care of her, then, mate," said Geoff.

He began to notice it more and more. Every time they met up away from home she actually looked younger and younger. There was something not right here. He would have to find out what she was doing. He decided to confide in Jake.

"You need to get yourself an iP760," said Jake.

They'd met in the King's Arms two hours ahead of Natural Atomic Time. The beer was tepid again. Shame. Clive actually liked real ale.

"What does that do, then?" asked Clive.

"It's got a tracking device. It can follow the whereabouts and the whenabouts of any other phone. You're really supposed to get the consent of owner, but, well, that's impossible to police and she wouldn't be able to give evidence against you in court."

"Aren't they expensive, though?" said Clive.

"There's a deal on at Rooney's this week," said. Jake. "Tell you what, sup up and I'll come with you to get one. I'll help you set it up, if you like."

He'd finally got the hang of it. The iP760 was even more complicated than the iP759. He'd managed to find her phone as well and connect the two while she wasn't looking in the brief time they'd spent together. But none of it was making any sense. According to what his communicator was telling him, she wasn't time travelling at all. Yet whenever they met up she was younger.

"Do you remember the first time we came here?" she asked when they met on the Burriana beach on their wedding anniversary.

Of course he did. She looked almost as young now as she had then. "Mmm," he mumbled. What was this? Was she trying to be romantic? That was long over, wasn't it?

She laughed. "You don't get it, do you?" she said. "You'd better take a look at this." She handed him what looked like a communicator but seemed very modern.

"What's this?" he said.

"You don't recognise it?" she said. "No, of course you wouldn't. It's a new sort of communicator."

"What…?"

"Check its history," she said. She laughed again and started running towards the sea. "You should go there. It's the only way you'll understand."

Clive felt faint when he saw where the communicator had come from. It would max out his time tranche allowance for a while. It would be an age before he built up enough credit to do very much at all. What had she been playing at? She was right, of course. He would have to go there. His hands shook as he copied the information from the old device to the new one.

There was the normal flash and then there he was standing outside what looked something like a technology shop, thirty years in the future. The one and only assistant, that Clive suspected was probably a droid and not human at all, was talking to an old woman who turned and waved at him. He suddenly felt self-conscious as he realised that his beachwear was both old-fashioned and inappropriate. Why is that old biddy being so friendly?

She came out of the shop. "You don't get it, do you?" she said. "I'm glad to see you got here, though."

There was something familiar about her face. Something horribly familiar and decidedly chilling.

"I have a month to live," she said. "I'm taking this back to just before where you'll land when your iP takes you back. I'll probably have less than a month in your timeline. Medicine wasn't so advanced then.

"I'm giving it to her, this iP995, so she can make an even better job of keeping out of your way than you are of keeping out of hers. Even though it means I won't be able to get back to my own time.

"See you around." She disappeared.

There was a flash and Clive was back on the beach. Miranda was still in the sea. Her bag was lying on the sun bed. He started to rummage inside. All he could find was her ordinary iP759.

A few minutes later she – Miranda – (which Miranda though?) strolled towards him.

"You won't find it there," she said. "And I wouldn't dream of letting you know where it really is." She sighed. She leant over and put her hands on his shoulders. She kissed him lightly on the forehead. "This is goodbye, I'm afraid. It's all set up so that our time paths will never cross again. Not when we're the right age at least. But she – I – will need you for the next month."

He wanted her to stay there. He wanted to breathe in the gentle perfume of her forever. He just wanted her full stop. It was like when they'd first met.

"Goodbye," she said. She gathered up her things and walked slowly away from him.

There was no point in following her.

"It's good to have you back," said Jake. "It must have been tough, having to watch someone die like that. But who was it exactly? You never said."

Clive took a sip of his lukewarm beer. It helped get rid of the lump in his throat.

"Just an old friend of the family," he said. "She was on her own. There was no one else."

"And the funeral was okay?"

"Yes. Fine. Though a bit sad as I was the only one there."

"Tough. Real tough. But what about Miranda?"

"That's over. Completely. She's just time travelling now."

"Well, you know, there is the new iP762. It can track anybody, any time."

Clive shook his head. "No, I'll never catch her," he said. "She's always one step ahead. And I don't want to meddle with that stuff anymore. It's nasty."

Jake sighed. "Up to you, mate."

The door of the King's Arms opened. Two people Clive had never met before came in.

"Ah yes," said Jake, "Suzy and Tom. Come and meet Clive." He turned back towards Clive. "We'll be sorting out the details for the spring tournament. People are so busy these days we won't be able to do it at all without the iP762s."

Clive finished his drink, stood up, nodded to Jake, Suzy and Tom and left. No more archery for him then.

Churches

"That's St Jude's. And that spire over there – can you see it? There? The black pointed one? That's St Bartholomew's. It's odd. It used to be Catholic."

"I thought they were mainly in the towns. And usually more modern."

"Yes. You're right. That's what makes St Bart's so strange. More the sort of place you'd have a quaint Anglican Church that's been there centuries."

"Which is older?"

"St Jude's of course. Notice the square stone tower."

Gary looked at where Lloyd was pointing. "I hope we never have to go there." They looked desolate, the people who had set up at St Jude's. The women wore dowdy headscarves and big frumpy skirts. The older men, the married men, they'd told him, grew beards and the younger ones wore old-fashioned braces over vest shirts. Clearly they had neither electricity nor any machines. It couldn't be much of a life.

"At least they're safe. And at least we know they're there if we really need them."

"Do you check out the route often?"

"At least once a week. You never know."

"You think it's that bad?"

Lloyd shrugged. "Well, let's not worry too much right now. Let's get back to the Hall."

There were several other four-by-fours already parked up at the Hall. Lloyd frowned. "Now what's up? Looks like we've got some visitors."

As Gary followed him into the office, his mouth went dry and his heart began to thud. He knew it was mistake leaving the town. Yes, the threat was ever present there but at least he was used to it. You could be all right in the countryside for months but when something went down, it did so dramatically and there was nowhere to run to. Well, maybe one place but that was hardly a great choice.

A young woman at the nearest computer terminal looked up at Lloyd and shook her head. "Cyber-attack. Massive. They've taken out all of our communication systems and we think the programmes operating the infra-structure will go down next."

"Have you called in help?"

"Yes, IBM, ASCA, Global Systems. It's too big for them even. These guys are getting really clever.

"May I?" Gary looked over at the girl's terminal. Code was eating itself. Yes, this was bad and there was little he could do, even with his expertise. He was the guy that IBM, ASCA and Global usually called in when they couldn't cope. Good, then, that he was already here. Bad, though, that it was useless.

The lights went out and all of the machines stopped.

"Can't we just drive out? Get back into the town? Wouldn't it be safer there?"

"No, we think they're surrounding us. According to what we've seen online."

The whirr of the generator stopped suddenly reminding him that the links to the outside were still tenuous. Yes, they had their own power now. Yes, they could connect to the outside world but many channels were still blocked and they were still fighting virus after virus.

"Do you want to come with me up to the tower? See what we can see?"

Gary nodded.

"Better wear this then." He handed Gary one of the black leather ANDROS jackets.

Gary slipped it on. The weight of it almost made him topple over.

Lloyd nodded. "It's bullet-proof of course."

God, this was a nightmare. Even so, a bit of fresh air at the top of the tower seemed welcome.

They made their way up the old stone spiral staircase. A breeze came down from the top. Gary drank in the clean air. He'd not realised how shut in he'd felt. To think he'd only agreed to this jaunt in order to escape the confines of the town. Now, he'd been more locked in than he would have been at home.

A girl in full defence uniform nodded to them when they got to the top.

"Any sign?" asked Lloyd.

She passed the binoculars to him. "On the edge of the woods. There's a patrol."

Lloyd nodded. He swung round and looked out to the farms. "And there are more of the bastards over there, look." He handed the binoculars to Gary.

He could see a group of men. Or were there women as well? They were all wearing caps with ear flaps but he saw no actual headscarves so he assumed they were all men. Surely any women belonging to the group would be orthodox and insist on covering their hair? Or, would non-orthodox women even consider joining HAMAL? Yes, men then. Brutish-looking men. The array of weapons was impressive. Pistols, rifles and strings of grenades. Even their bullet-proof vests looked as if they might actually be bombs. Why were the authorities allowing this? Why weren't they stamping on it?

He knew the answer if he was honest: not enough man-power. It was pretty much every one for themselves these days.

"We think we've seen them putting down landmines along the trunk road." The girl pointed to the main road leading from the farm. "Cutting across the fields would be impossible. We'd be too exposed. Any offer of negotiation?"

Lloyd shook his head. "They're not communicating with us."

The girl pursed her lips and raised her eyebrows. "We're scuppered, I guess."

"That's all we've got left now?" Lloyd was looking into the opened ten kilo bag of potatoes. He pulled one out. It didn't exactly look appetizing. It was wrinkled and growing tubers. There was another unopened bag next to it. "That will keep us going for a day and a half. Tops."

"If the water holds out. The generator's playing up again." The kitchen operative had obviously been tinkering with it. His white overalls were smeared with oil.

Right on cue the soft whirr of the machine stopped.

The operative tutted. "Here we go again. Don't hold your breath."

Gary realised he wasn't going to get out of this. They wouldn't be able get to one of the churches, surrounded as they were. What sort of death would it be exactly? Slow, by starvation, or sudden, by terrorist attack?

God, if only he'd stayed in the town. He'd got wits enough to survive there. He was used to that.

"Come on," said Lloyd. "I want to show you something."

"Just make sure there's no one coming and then shut the door."

They were in the hardly used morning room. It was old and its oak panelling was delicate. They wanted to preserve it in case one day everything went back to normal. It was a bit of beautiful history worth hanging on to if they ever had a future.

Lloyd touched the top of the wooden panel next to the great mantelpiece. A door sprung open, making Gary jump. "Blimey. Secret passage or what?"

Lloyd nodded. "Priest hole. Yes, there is a secret passage behind it. It leads to St Bart's."

"I didn't think St Bart's was old enough for that."

"Ah, but it is actually. Only the spire is relatively new."

"So, why haven't we evacuated before?"

Lloyd sighed. "Once you've joined the church there's no way back. If you stay outside there's always the hope that we might get the better of them."

"We won't though, will we?" Of course he knew the answer to that. He knew as well that even if he'd stayed in the town they would have got him eventually. He just might have been a bit more comfortable for a bit longer.

Lloyd shook his head. "Coming then?"

"What about the others? Didn't you tell them?"

"Too risky. If too many of us disappear in one go they'll probably attack."

"But you're leaving them all to die."

"We'll leave the door to the passage open. Perhaps they'll find it. Hopefully they'll be sensible enough only to follow in small groups. Shall we?"

He followed Lloyd into the gloom.

Ten minutes in, Gary's eyes had got used to the dark and he could see well enough that he didn't have to keep holding on to the wall. The ground underfoot was surprisingly firm. "So has this been used recently?"

"Well, I did a dummy run as soon as I found out about it. That puzzled me too. It was almost as if it had been made ready for us. Deliberately."

"You don't think it's some sort of trap, do you? You don't think they've set us up?"

"Would they dare? It leads to a church, after all."

Gary decided it was best not to think about it too much. Better just to concentrate on putting one foot in front of the other. The passageway was getting narrower now and he had the sensation that they were going down. They would have to go back up at some point. St Bart's was higher than the Hall.

It was getting colder and the air was musty now. "How much further is it?"

"We're just over half way."

The passage seemed to swing up now. There was source of light ahead of them.

Lloyd put his hand up, signalling that they should stop. Then he put a finger to his lips.

Gary could hear voices. They were speaking a language he didn't understand. Extremists, he supposed. Were they in the passage?

At last Lloyd gave the signal that they could carry on. "There's a way out into the woods there. I made sure it was hidden from the outside a few weeks back. Thank God. I don't think they realise it's there. Come on. Not far now."

The air began to sweeten again. The passage swung up steeply and soon they faced a door. Lloyd pushed it open and they made their way up a set of steep stone steps. Another door led them into what must be the crypt of St Bart's.

The door wouldn't open at first but gave suddenly after Lloyd had pushed it hard with his shoulder several times. Gary heard a startled scream.

They came face to face with one of the strangely dressed girls.

"We're seeking asylum," said Lloyd quickly.

"Of course," said the girl. "You made me jump. I didn't even know there was a door there."

"Sorry."

She smiled and all at once Gary could see beyond the shapeless clothes and the dowdy greying head scarf. She had the most beautiful dark brown eyes. "You are very welcome. Come, I'll introduce you to the Elders."

Gary closed the door behind him and noticed that it disappeared completely. It looked now just like another of the painted panels. Clever, these Catholics.

He thought the girl seemed a little nervous. She played with the huge crucifix hanging round her neck and a couple of times put it to her lips and kissed it gently. Was this some sort of religious ritual?

He guessed he'd better try and get used to it. The days of worshiping technology were over now. That had always been his religion. He supposed he'd better get used to this new one.

"It's all right. She won't hurt you." Gary was working with Miriam, the girl they met when they first arrived. She had been assigned as his mentor. They were harvesting leeks and were right at the edge of the Compound. Just a few feet away on the other side of the fence was one of the extremists. Over the top of her full burka she wore a wired vest. Eyes just as dark and as beautiful as Miriam's stared into theirs.

Miriam nodded to the girl. Something that might have been a smile lit up the girl's eyes slightly. Then she turned and walked away.

Miriam touched his arm gently. "Don't be scared. The vests are just for show. That near to us, at least. They respect the churches. We have Abraham in common."

She put down her trowel. She tapped her crucifix. "I must come clean," she said. "I'm actually Jewish, not Christian at all. But we still have Abraham. And the churches."

Gary nodded. Thank God for the churches.

107

Bright Soldiers Marching

"It will be fine," says Marten. "If he wakes we'll play." He touches my arm. "He knows me well enough."

Of course I'm nervous about more than Richard waking. This is such a big thing that we're attempting. And I should trust Marten. He's been such a friend since Klemm died.

He pushes me lightly towards the door. "Go on. Go and get her."

I get out of the car and make my way over to the Kindergarten. I open the heavy wooden door. Fräulein Mensen is already making her way towards me, holding Liliane firmly by the wrist. Liliane is dragging her feet.

"Here she is, already for her Oma's birthday party." Fräulein Mensen smiles.

I can see they have put her in her best party frock as I requested. Hopefully this subterfuge will work. Well, she looks the part.

She stamps her foot. "I don't want to go to a party. Anyway, Oma had her birthday just after mine. It can't be her birthday again."

"That was her saint's day," I say.

Thank goodness for Catholic saints' days. And thank goodness I've remembered that. One advantage of our conversion to Catholicism. It didn't entirely work, though, or we wouldn't be having to do this.

Fräulein Mensen raises an eyebrow. Does she believe me?

I grab Liliane's hand and start to pull her towards the door.

"Stop it, you're hurting." She pulls back. "I want a wee-wee. Please, Mutti, I want a wee-wee."

"Can't you wait until we get to Oma's?"

She shakes her head. Well, it is a bit much to expect. Especially since we're actually not going to Oma's. Even a grown-up would be pushed to control their bladder for the distance we have to cover. I expect there will be a few stops to crouch behind bushes.

I open the door to the bathroom.

Instead of going straight to the toilet, though, she stares at herself in the mirror. The corner of her mouth twitches into the suggestion of a smile. Vanity at her age! We don't need this right now.

"For goodness sake, get on with it," I shout, pulling her drawers down and lifting her on to the seat. She begins to whimper.

Fräulein Mensen appears at the doorway. I try to smile at her. "We're in such a hurry. Her brother's outside in the car with Herr Goldbaum. I don't want us to be late."

Fräulein Mensen flinches a little at the name Goldbaum. Well, of course it's the same name as Klemm's. Marten is his brother after all.

Liliane finishes peeing. She did want to go. She wasn't faking it. I hand her a couple of sheets of toilet paper. She wipes herself and I flush the toilet. She admires herself again as she washes her hands. I stroke her head and kiss her on the cheek. "Yes, you do look lovely in that dress. Oma will love you for it." I really should have more patience with her.

She giggles.

I hate myself for the lies I'm telling.

"Okay, let's go," says Marten.

Liliane snuggles down into the seat next to Michael. He stirs a little but doesn't wake up.

"You do look gorgeous," Marten says as he pulls out. "Your Oma will be impressed."

Liliane gasps. "Mutti, do we have a present for Oma?"

Marten and I look at each other in his mirror. He bites his lip.

"We're going to stop and buy her some flowers at that shop she likes in the village," I say.

"Oh. Can I choose?"

I nod. "Yes. Why don't you have a little nap until we get there?"

"Okay."

Just a few moments later we hear her gentle snoring harmonizing beautifully with her brother's.

Marten puts a hand on mine. "Good that they're both asleep. We should make good progress before they wake up. And then maybe we can tell them what's really happening. Hopefully by then we'll be far enough away."

He squeezes my hand and then puts his own back on the steering wheel. I wish he'd left his hand on mine. And I wish I didn't get those shivers of excitement every time he touches me. It's too soon after Klemm. We have too much else to think about at the moment. I have no idea, anyway, if he feels the same way. I'm not sure I can face the disappointment if he doesn't.

I envy the children their sleep. They seem to have no cares at all.

"You should try to sleep for a bit as well," says Marten.

See, he can read my thoughts. Sleep is the last thing I think I'll manage, though.

"Go on," he says. "Shut your eyes. You need the rest."

I obey. It's still part of my nature always to do what the menfolk say.

He's right. It is surprisingly relaxing having my eyes shut and feeling the gentle motion of the car. Marten is a good driver.

I must have drifted off to sleep because suddenly I wake up

and the sun is really low. The car has stopped. We seem to be in a queue. Michael is standing up and tapping Marten's shoulder vigorously. "Can we go and see them, Onkel Marten? Can we go and see them, please?"

Liliane is just waking. She rubs her eyes and frowns.

"Are we at Oma's yet? It's taking a long time."

"We've had to come a different way round because of the soldiers," says Marten.

"Soldiers?" I say. My mouth goes dry and my heart starts to thud.

"They're on their way to the Sudetenland, I guess," says Marten.

"Please can we go and see them. Please." Michael is getting quite red in the face now.

"I don't see why not," says Marten. He pulls the car over to the kerb and takes the key from the ignition.

"Are you mad?" I whisper.

"It's the most natural thing to do. Look." He points to the cars in front of us. Everyone is getting out.

"I don't like soldiers," says Liliane.

"You've got to come with us. We can't leave you in the car." I don't tell her, of course, that I agree completely. If we didn't have soldiers we wouldn't have wars.

Marten takes Michael's hand and I take Liliane's. Marten put his free arm around my waist and propels us through the crowds. "We're good German citizens, supporting our brave young men," he whispers. His lips almost touch my ear. I want him to kiss me.

We find a space in the crowds. Marten hoists Michael on to his shoulders. I hold Liliane in front of me.

There are thousands of them. First the young men holding the flags. The red and black symbol fills me with dread. It looks like the cogged wheel of some great machine that will plough us into the ground. Then there are the

111

soldiers in their tin hats and marching with their goose steps. The noise is terrifying. Their boots clatter on the road and the crowds cheer and chant. Some of the women throw flowers at these husbands, brothers, sons and fiancés. Yes, I know that's what they are, but all I can see are soldiers.

"Bright soldiers marching!" cries Michael, jigging up and down.

Marten winces then grins. "Yes, bright soldiers marching."

Liliane grabs my hand and puts her thumb in her mouth. She scowls.

The tanks are the worst. They rumble past and at any moment I expect one of the guns to turn and blow me to oblivion.

"They're just doing their job. They have to," he whispers.

I know this. I really do. But I can't feel it.

At last they have gone past. We make our way back to the car.

"The flower shop will be shut," says Liliane.

"Your Oma will understand when we tell her about the soldiers," says Marten.

"I hope they've saved us some cake," says Michael.

Marten laughs. "Of course they will have."

I hate these lies.

We continue the journey in silence. It grows dark. The children are wide awake but they say nothing. Marten is getting tired, I think.

"Do you want to stop for a while?" I ask.

"No, I just want to get there."

Liliane says nothing. I was expecting her to protest at any moment that we've gone too far to be going to Oma's. I'm sure she knows. She must do.

"This bit will be rough," says Marten at last. "And I daren't have the lights on. You might have to get out occasionally and guide me."

I nod. Still the children are silent. They just stare. Goodness knows what they're thinking. We daren't tell them anything yet, though. Not until we're across the border.

We travel on up a track that goes between the trees. Twice I have to get out to open and shut gates across farmland. And twice more to hold the torch down to the ground.

"We're not going to see Oma, are we?" says Liliane.

I turn and touch her cheek. "No, sweetheart. We're not. I'm sorry I lied to you."

"I won't see my friends again, will I?"

"No," says Marten, "but you will make new ones. You'll see."

We arrive at a normal road at last. Before we turn on to it, Marten stops the engine.

"Come on," he says. "Let's look at our new country."

We can't see much because it's so dark. We deliberately chose a night when there would be no moonlight. "You'll see the windmills when it's daylight. You'll love the light here. It reflects off the water. The people here are kind. We'll be safe."

He puts his arm round my waist and kisses the top of my head. I want to turn my face up to him, to kiss him on the lips. I don't know whether he wants me to, though.

"Are you going to be our new daddy?" asks Michael.

Marten laughs. "I don't know about that but I will most certainly care for my brother's widow and his children. That's normal."

He pulls me to him. "Welcome to your new home and your new way of life," he whispers.

I feel safe.

Faceless

Von activated the scanner again. It made another full pass through the brain of the deep-sleeper on the operating table. Same as before. Nothing. Not even an outline. The trauma must have been particularly bad.

Normally Von liked the clinical calm of the windowless lab. It was just her and the hum of the scanners and life-support machines. Today, though, it was disturbing her. She couldn't work out why, other than that this was a particularly difficult case. She had company as well.

"Still no good?" Dan Fletcher always liked to hang around until Von and her scanners could give him a picture of who'd committed the crime. He was often a bit of a nuisance actually but this time he might just be useful. "Do you reckon she's understood the questions?"

Von shrugged. Had their language or the human brain for that matter changed that much in 250 years? A 23rd century brain would always respond well to the probes. Anyway the probes didn't use language as such. They triggered emotional responses.

"You're sure it's not your readers that are wrong? Surely they didn't have deep-sleep technology back then? It wasn't invented until thirty years ago, was it?"

"That's what we thought," muttered Von. Why did he always have to know better? "But she's definitely in deep-sleep and she's definitely 250 years old." Her machinery was the best. There was no chance of there being an error.

"Even better than Sleeping Beauty. She only managed 100 years." He pulled a face at the woman on the table. "Except she ain't no beauty."

He was right there. She was so thin her ribs showed. Her arms looked as if they would snap if you as much as touched them. Her head was just a skull thinly wrapped in skin. Her mouth was slightly open, showing that she had several teeth missing. Well, there was always some atrophy in deep-sleep. Maybe it was more acute after such a long time. Would the high-protein and vitamin drips be enough to restore her? Her body certainly seemed to be absorbing them rapidly.

"Tell me again where and how did you find her?"

Dan shook his head. "East section 156."

"There's nothing out there, is there?"

"Not any more. We had to go in radiation suits. Just in case."

"But she's safe?" No radiation at all had shown up on the scan.

"Yeah. In fact the whole area's clean now."

"Really?"

Dan nodded.

It was impossible. There should have still been fall-out from the accident. Had anything actually happened there then? Or had it been some sort of cover-up?

The atrophy of the deep-sleeper and the mystery about the lack of radiation kept going round in Von's mind that night. She hated losing sleep. There was nothing for it than to get up and see if she could find out any more.

She was hardly surprised when a search on East section 156 revealed that she was entering a restricted information area. There was very little there – except about the accident in 2134. Nothing much about what was there. Nothing about – Edith's time.

Edith? Where had that come from? They didn't normally name the deep-sleepers. They did that themselves sooner or later. Had she read something yesterday? A fleeting glimpse, maybe?

Von's heart was beating wildly as she typed in "Edith, East section 156."

Something sprang up on the screen. A picture of a woman, gaunt like – Edith. No hair. Overalls.

Then it disappeared.

"We are sorry to terminate your connection. You are entering an area of restricted information. Please do not attempt that search again."

Von sighed. This was useless. Still, if it was restricted information, didn't that prove that there was something a bit suspicious about the area? And anyway – Edith, shaved head, overalls – it might be worth a try.

She went back to bed and straight to sleep.

She was beginning to colour up nicely now. The drips must be doing their work. Her lips were softening too. Already the dental team had made the preparations for implants. By the time she came round her mouth would be quite used to them.

"Well, Edith, you're beginning to look human. But your scans are still not telling me anything." They only showed the low-level motor activity that was keeping her alive. "I wish you could tell me something."

One of the scanner's lights flickered. Von read the output. Left frontal AP147. Recognition. Was it possible that she knew her name? That she'd heard it and remembered it?

Von knew she had to be careful. They must always guard against creating ideas in the minds of their patients. Even so, this one was blank. The other problem might be that the sleeper could awake with a still completely dysfunctional mind.

"I wish I knew who you were and who had done this to you." Most of the deep-sleepers had pre-set reawakening times and all about them was catalogued. Even the few criminal cases carried more information that this one.

116

Von looked more closely at the sleeper. Now that she had plumped and coloured up a little she looked quite young. Maybe the hair was ash blond rather than grey after all.

The woman moved her fingers. She grumbled faintly. Was she waking already? Von looked at the scanner. Nothing. Yet there was obviously something going on.

It was tempting. She knew she shouldn't do it. It was only allowed in coma patients and then only if you knew exactly who they were and what their background was. But what if she hooked herself up to Edith? What if she thought of that picture she had glimpsed? It was only a shadow of an image after all and Edith would recognise it as such if she were that conscious. Could it be anyway that her mind was so blank after all this time that any stimulus would do something? If she was found out, that's how she would explain it.

Her mouth was dry as she attached the probe. She concentrated hard and thought about the young woman she had seen.

Edith murmured and started moving her head from side to side. She seemed to be receiving the message. Would she send something back?

Von flicked the scanner into receive mode and watched the screen. Nothing happened at first. Then something started to appear – much more slowly than usual. Was it a face? Something was emerging. A shadow was growing. Normally a face would appear in about ten seconds. This time after a full two minutes later there was only the suggestion of an outline.

It was indeed a face appearing, though.

Slowly, slowly the chin appeared. Then the cheekbones. The forehead. Gradually more details appeared. A nose, ears, a small thin mouth. And last the eyes. Cold eyes that made Von shudder.

Edith started thrashing around violently. She whimpered.

"What's scaring you, then?" Von placed her hand on Edith's arm and rubbed it gently. The sleeper calmed a little.

The face was quite clear now. Something about it that made Von shudder. And it seemed familiar.

The cold eyes stared and made her more and more uncomfortable. The lips began to move. It was trying to speak.

Edith was still now.

Dare she directly reverse probe her mind now? That was frowned upon as well. Yet it seemed it was the only way she would find out more about this woman. And also, maybe, something about the face. He had stopped talking now.

She would do it. She trembled as she reattached the probe and typed the instructions.

The face stayed still.

Then he was standing there in front of her. He looked like a doctor. Yes, he had a stethoscope around his neck. He was coming towards her, trying to take her hand. She was afraid. Why was she afraid? Doctors were good, weren't they? Not this one, though. Thick eyebrows. Very thick. Intense eyes. They seemed to pierce right into her. He was wearing a uniform. His hat his was tipped slightly to the side. He grinned and waved the hypodermic needle at her.

She looked round the room at the others. They averted their eyes. The pregnant women put her hand on her large belly. How could someone that thin sustain a pregnancy? She knew though that the woman was expecting twins and that was why the good doctor was so interested. How did she know that? It must have been Edith's memory.

"Come on. Let's do this thing," he whispered. "It's that or the gas chamber."

"Don't touch me, angel of death." She pushed him hard.

"Bitch." He jabbed the needle into her arm.

It all went black.

Von jumped. The probe slipped off. "Mengele," she whispered. Where did that come from? Was that Edith's real name? Or the doctor's? She looked at the screen. The face had dissolved again and now she couldn't quite remember what it had looked like. She just sensed evil.

Whatever had happened to Edith must have been bad. Very bad. And it would be cruel to make anyone remember that.

Von knew what she must do.

"So, it wasn't viable, then?"

Von shook her head. Couldn't get any readings. The stimulants wouldn't wake her."

Dan Fletcher shrugged. "Sounds like it was a very primitive attempt at deep-sleep then. How far did you get?"

"Level three. Then she seemed to have a sudden cardiac arrest."

"Did you try the defib?"

"Yes. And I used the internal paddles. Nothing." She didn't of course mention the air she'd injected into Edith's blood stream.

"Ah well. We'll never know. They probably had no idea how to set it up properly in those days. Shame they'd already done the dental work."

Dan slipped on his jacket and left.

Von smiled to herself as she saw the smoke coming from the crematorium. Edith's body had gone now. Nobody would ever know.

Lady in Blue

The air con made her thin blue skirt dance. She shivered. She moved away from the door. Tonight she would attach herself just for a short while to the man and woman and their two children. She was aware of the young couple watching her. They were both drinking huge gin and tonics. The ice filled the tall glasses.

"There's no room for the tonic," she heard the young woman say.

The family didn't seem to see her. It wouldn't be the first time. They were busy. She was dowdy.

The clock struck nine. The young couple moved towards the restaurant. The family moved towards their hotel room. She moved towards the garden. She wandered between the flower beds and tutted as one of the sprinklers sprayed water at her skirt.

All of the tables were already taken.

"I thought they didn't open until nine," the young woman muttered.

"It's all right," said the head waiter. "We can set up another table." He set to, rolling the table from the store to the front of the garden. He fetched a table-cloth, some cutlery and some glasses. "There," he said. He made a big show of opening the menus for them. "Tonight's special is lamb, roast with thyme."

"Mm. That sounds delicious," said the young woman.

The waiter nodded. Then she was standing face to face with him. The woman in the blue skirt. "Could I have a table for one?" she said.

"I don't know..." He'd understood her French, no problem. He probably didn't like that damp patch on her skirt.

"You know you must," she said in Spanish.

It did the trick. Just about. He shook his head, muttered something and wandered back towards the garden store. A few moments later her table was ready. "Can I get you something to drink?" he asked.

"Just a glass of water for now. Tap water."

"Your companion's coming, this time, is he?"

"Of course."

The waiter came back with some bread. The young couple ordered. Their food came. Still no sign of Jeffrey. She sipped the water. She crumbled the bread on to the table and made patterns with it. She thought about the family who had been in the bar. They'd been eating burgers and French fries. What dull food. And how miserable it had been in there with the over-zealous air con. It was much nicer out here. When Jeffrey arrived they would order something delicious. Maybe the roast lamb.

Another couple with a grown-up daughter arrived at the table next to hers. They were French as well. They looked as if they'd just been travelling. Perhaps there was a lot of traffic.

She walked over to them and introduced herself. "I'm waiting for my husband. We stayed here on our honeymoon," she explained. "We were on our way to the Costa del Sol. I was wondering. Was the traffic bad?"

The man shook his head. "Not so bad really. We were held up a little in Madrid. Our daughter was at a photo-shoot there." He grinned at the young girl by his side.

She giggled. "You always exaggerate, Papa."

"I have every right to be proud of you, my dear."

"So why are you meeting your husband here?" asked the woman. "Why didn't you come together?"

"It's what we arranged. It's been arranged for years."

"Oh." The woman looked puzzled.

"Only he's very late. I'm worried."

"I'm sure he'll be here soon. The traffic's not too bad. We had the radio on all the way. There haven't been any accidents. Try not to worry."

She leant forward and air-kissed the woman twice. "Vous êtes très gentille, madame."

She went back to her table. It was getting really dark now. She could see two of the waiters looking at her. They were whispering. Were they going to call the police again?

The young woman seemed to be looking at her. Oh yes. Her skirt was damp. She'd caught it in the sprinkler again as she'd crossed the garden.

She shivered. Again? What did she mean again? She was waiting for Jeffrey, wasn't she? As arranged. All that time ago. Wait. Why had they arranged to meet here? Why so long ago?

The waiter came over to her table again. "Are you going to order? Is your companion coming this time?"

"He'll come. I'm sure he'll come."

The waiter shook his head and moved away muttering. Why did they always have to be so rude?

What did he mean "this time"? She had arranged to meet Jeffrey here. Now.

The waiters were talking about her, she could see. So were the two young people. I couldn't help walking into the sprinkler, she thought. It could happen to anyone.

Yet she had the feeling that this had happened before.

She felt afraid suddenly. Would the police come again in their cars with their sirens? Would they shout at her, order her away? Brutally, like they did the last time.

She stuffed the bread into her handbag and got up purposefully from her seat. "I don't think he's coming," she called to the waiter. "He'll be here tomorrow, I'm sure."

"No he won't," she heard the waiter mutter. "Nor the next day, nor the one after that."

The garden began to fade. She felt light-headed.

She would come back tomorrow. Jeffrey would come tomorrow. She was sure.

Mantek's Journey

Charlek was lying amongst the horses' straw. His face was grey, his lips blue. I knelt down beside him. I could feel his breath on my cheek. Prince, the Master's latest stallion, was pawing nervously at the ground.

Charlek stirred a little. He grabbed my tunic and pulled me towards him, until my ear was level with his mouth.

"You must… you must," he struggled to say. "You must go with the Master. To where the star is taking him." He made the sign of blessing on my forehead. He took in a long rasping breath. His chest rattled and then he was silent.

"Is he… is he?" asked Zarib.

I nodded. I had seen a man die once before. My father, too, had collapsed just like that.

So, I was now to be in charge of the stable boys and oversee the grooming of the Master's fine horses. I was secretly pleased. Not that Charlek had died, you understand – he had been a good friend – but that I could take on this new responsibility. I had dreamt for a long time of being in charge of a stable. I was capable of the task, too. I was fond of Charlek. But his death had at least saved me seeking a new position.

We carried Charlek to his final resting place on a cool clear day. The Master attended but said very little. He did not join in our singing and dancing at the wake. Before he went back to his quarters, he drew me aside.

"Come to me when the celebration is over," he said.

I went to him that evening. I had never been so close to the Master before. He normally preferred his own company. He had no wife and no children and was never seen with a companion. I gawped at how much taller and younger he looked close to. His beard must have made him seem older before.

I had never been to his rooms. They were like nothing I had ever seen. The walls were covered in blue and red silks. There were thick mats on the floor and the room was furnished with soft chairs and sofas. The Master himself was also clothed in fine silks and satins.

He was looking out of the window through a long tube when I came in. He must have heard me, for he spoke though he did not turn to look at me.

"Mantek. Good, you are here," he said. "We are to go on a journey." He still looked out of the window and not directly at me. "Does that suit you, Mantek?"

I didn't know what to say. I had just taken charge of the stable. I didn't want to leave. I wanted to prove I could run everything as well as Charlek had, if not better.

"You are very quiet, Mantek," he said. "Does the idea of travelling not please you?"

I still could not speak.

Then he turned to me. "Come," he said, gesturing that I should join him at the window. He pointed towards the sky. "Do you see that star? The one in the East? Brighter than the rest?"

I looked to where he was pointing. I didn't know much about the stars, but I could see that this one was shining more brightly than those around it.

"It is a new star," the Master continued. "We've been waiting for it for hundreds of years."

Now he looked deeply into my eyes.

"Only three of us will go," he said. "I shall take only two men I can trust. You are one of those men, Mantek. I know you will look after my horses well. Now go, and prepare yourself and six fine horses for the journey."

I was flattered. Not many fifteen-year-olds are spoken to as equals by men older than them, let alone by someone as wise and as rich as our Master. But that did not stop me feeling worried about the journey. Good as I was with the horses, I wasn't sure I could look after them properly away from the comfortable stable. And I was sure that all too soon the Master would find out I was no more than a boy when my competence or my courage, or both, failed.

Two days later we set off at dusk. The star shone brightly even then. We planned to travel mainly by night, so that we could always see the star. I believe it was actually so bright we would have still been able to see it during the day.

All went well at first. I was pleased that I had chosen the right horses. Each day we rode three and three carried our extra supplies. Archamid, the longest-serving of the Master's other servants, accompanied us. The horses were well-behaved and strong. We made good progress, though I was not sure exactly where we were going. The Master talked to Archamid as though he were a friend and not a servant at all. They said little to me, and I was left to my own thoughts. But they didn't treat me like a boy and they showed me every respect when they wanted to know about the animals. I was the expert then. I was allowed to do everything for the horses on my own. Except that the master always insisted in packing his own things. Every evening I saw him place very carefully into his saddlebag something wrapped in several pieces of cloth.

We slept by day. It was warm then and we could get snug in our tents. I was much better cared for there than I was at home: the stable master always sleeps in the stables with the horses. Here, the horses were kept outside the tents and my tent was as fine as those of Archamid's and the Master's.

But on the third evening the trouble began.

Archamid was frowning.

"This sand gets everywhere," he said, shaking some

from out of his boot. "We shall look like tramps by the time we find what the star wants to show us." He complained all the time. It was too cold. The saddle was making him sore. He had no idea where we were going.

The Master said nothing but continued to stare at the star.

By the fourth evening Archamid was even more restless.

"I'm too old for this sort of journey," he complained. "I should be resting in the comfort of my own little home at my age." For the rest of that night there were even more moans and groans from him.

Still the Master said nothing. I wanted to argue with Archamid, and tell him he was being selfish, but my Master's solemn silence would not let me.

On the fifth evening, just as the sun was getting low in the sky and we were loading the horses ready to leave, Archamid started again.

"What will we do when we find the star's final resting place?" he asked. "Will we find riches there, fit to bring back to our families?"

"There will be no treasure that you will recognise," said the Master softly.

"What?" cried Archamid. "You are dragging us away from our homes? And there will be no return?" His face was red with anger.

"What you find there will be greater than treasure but you will not be able to pick it up and carry it," said the Master, again speaking calmly.

"You are fooling me," said Archamid.

The Master smacked Tangent's rump hard.

The fine horse bolted, along with Archamid's belongings.

I wanted to gallop out and retrieve the animal. I

mounted Starcrest, his brother, ready to follow. The Master stopped me with the wave of his arm.

"You go and retrieve your belongings," said the Master to Archamid, "as material goods are so important to you."

Archamid jumped on Snow and followed Tangent. We watched them disappear into the distance.

"They will not be back," said the Master. "They are lost to us forever, and I fear that Archamid has lost himself, too, and it will be difficult for him to find the right path again. But you will continue on the journey with me?" he asked.

I nodded. Two of my good horses were lost. I must stay with the other four. "How much longer will it take?" I asked.

The Master looked up at the sky for a few minutes.

"Ten more days, I think," he said.

I too looked at the star. It was even brighter and bigger than before. I thought it might explode.

We travelled on. The Master did not say much. I occupied myself with the four remaining horses. They covered the miles well. We became used to just following the star. I soon learnt to forget the noises of the day. I relished each dawn the softness of my feather mattress and the comfort of the smooth silk sheets pulled over me. It was easy, really, to sleep in the heat in our cool tents. I always took care to find shade for the horses too.

On the thirteenth night, the star seemed even closer and brighter. The Master stared at it constantly and seemed in a trance. I wondered whether it might be the gentle movement of the horses which had lulled him into his dream state. But I did not feel rocked to sleep. I was wide awake with the stirrings of some great expectation. I had no idea what was to happen, but I sensed the importance of these times.

The sun came slowly up. We made camp as usual. I tied

the horses and gave them food and water. The supplies were dwindling, but the Master assured me we would be able to find enough at our destination for the return journey. I gave the animals their full ration and then started to cook a meal for the Master and myself.

"Mantek!" the Master called suddenly. "Listen."

I heard nothing at first. Then there was a sound. A rustling amongst the trees.

"Take up arms!" shouted the Master.

Two men appeared from the nearby bushes. They had shining swords. I had no weapon on me and although the Master wore a sword, he made no attempt to use it. The rough-looking men jumped at him. He moved his right arm quickly and the taller of the two men bowled over, as if struck by a hard rock. The second charged at the Master who raised his staff which seemed to almost decapitate the shorter of the two men, who let out a piercing cry. The Master looked white with fury. The second rushed forward again, but the Master repelled him as well with the staff. The would-be thief hurtled into our water jug. There was a loud crack. The last of our water trickled on to the sandy ground and disappeared at once. The two men, shaken and bruised, crawled away, muttering curses at my Master. We were safe. But we had no water.

"Do you think we shall hold out?" I asked. "Can we really go any further without water?"

"We have just two more days' sleep and two more nights' to travel," replied the Master. "The Power of the Star will protect us for this time."

He seemed to believe what he was saying. But I was doubtful. The day-time heat became too fierce as we travelled eastwards and though it was much cooler at night, our bodies needed fluids.

We slept for the rest of that day. The next evening when

I saddled the horses, I worried about their lack of water.

"Please forgive me," I whispered to Stardust and Prince, to Chaser and Gallant. "There is no water tonight." I'm not sure what those dumb animals thought, but they seemed to appreciate me talking to them. Prince nuzzled my face and all four neighed softly.

At first it was not too bad. We made good progress and I did not feel thirsty. The star shimmered and glistened before us. It carried on becoming brighter and bigger as it had every night. Now, the whole of the Eastern sky was alight.

Then, just before day break, there came a change, however, and I do not know to this day whether it was the lack of water making me hallucinate or whether the whole sky really was filled with men-like creatures that had great feathered wings. They seemed to be made of light. There was sound. Voice music, such as I had never heard before and have never heard since. The Master seemed to move in slow motion. He mouthed something to me, but I could not make out what he said.

I don't remember stopping to sleep. I do remember waking the next evening. The Master was shaking me.

"Mantek," he said – I could hear him now, for he was very close to me – "Are you going to sleep all night? Do you not want to see the King's glory?"

We continued through the last night. The sky was still ablaze with light. I could still hear the singing, but could no longer make out the shapes of the men with wings. There was just light, more and more light. We arrived at a small town. The Master spoke to a woman. They seemed to talk for a long time, and she did not look best pleased. Eventually, she led us to a well. We drank. Then, I filled a trough for the horses. They weren't as thirsty as I expected, though they did make noises which I thought told me they were glad of the water. The sun would soon be up. The light faded from the sky, leaving the star shining brilliantly against a now dark sky. It seemed to point to a low building, a stable perhaps. How odd. Hadn't the Master said something about a King?

He spoke again to the woman – I couldn't understand what they said – the people there did not speak our language. She pointed towards the building over which the star shone.

Strangely, the horses seemed to know what to do. With no command from me, they moved steadily towards the building which looked less and less like the home of a King the nearer we got to it. I didn't trust the women. I thought she was out to trick us and they we would once again be attacked by thieves – maybe her brothers.

But more and more people were making their way to the same place. If we were being tricked, we weren't the only ones. The Master seemed to know all the other travellers. Some rode on camels, others on horses, and some as fine as our own, some less so. They all appeared to be bringing gifts – fine linens, spices, ointments. At last the Master took out what he had kept so closely guarded in Prince's saddlebag – a large nugget of the purest gold.

We all moved silently. We did not speak as we approached the birth place of the King. But later, after we had seen the babe, my Master conversed for hours with the other Sages and Wiseman. Again I could not understand what they said but I could tell they were excited to exchange their wisdom about the event.

In the stable we found an ordinary woman and her man, and the baby. He had no crib, nor fine clothes fit for a king. He had no servant, just this older man who I could not believe was his father. But I don't think I have ever seen such a serene child or such a radiant mother. The light

131

which shone from their faces was brighter even than that of the star and of whatever else I saw in the skies above. This child was a bringer of peace. That much was clear. I just knew it, even though no one told me. Tiny baby that he was, his eyes held mine for a split second and I know he could see right into me, and he understood everything about me. Understood, me yes – and this is going to sound a bit crazy – no very crazy – he forgave me for the mistakes I've made. Now, he only looked at me for a few seconds, but we understood each other in that time, me and him.

And here were all these wise men, kings in their own right, bowing down before him. We all knew He was going to bring peace to this world. How, I could not imagine, especially from this small place, but as soon as I looked at him, all desire left me and I felt only deep contentment.

On the way out of the town we met the woman who had taken us to the well and shown us the way to the stable. She spoke for a few minutes to my Master.

"Do you know that woman used to be a prostitute?" said the Master after we'd waved goodbye to her. "That's why she was wary of us – she thinks all men want only one thing. But she's just told me she will never go back on the game. One look from that Holy Child was enough."

Just as one look, just as it had been for me. It didn't last forever, of course. The rest of my life has not been without its ups and downs, and there has been plenty of agitation with a wife and five daughters to feed and tolerate. But I often think back to the time we followed the star and then I am filled with a delightful calm.

On the way home, the Master told me of the great prophecy that said a Prince of Peace would be born under that star. We've heard a little of that Holy Child since. He too has become a man and he performs miracles and tells the priests in his country their business. We had a miracle,

I think, on the way home. Our horses travelled lightly. We took five days less to get home than we had taken to go there. We ran out of neither grain nor water. Nor did we meet any thieves.

I think I was meant to see that child. God forgive me, but I think that's why Charlek had his heart attack. He went in peace and I think he knew. That's why he gave me his blessing.

The First Pot-Luck Supper

"Oh, go on, let him go," said Zac's father. "He's worked really hard lately. We can spare him for a day."

Zac's mother was frowning. Zac knew that all the talk about finishing the new furniture for the innkeeper's widow was just one big excuse. She simply didn't want him to go and listen to the Master. He couldn't understand what she was so afraid of. After all, the new teacher was just an ordinary sort of person – in fact, the son of carpenter, just like he was.

She sighed.

"All right then," she said, "but you'd better take something to eat with you."

"Oh, Mum!" said Zac, frustrated. There would be bound to be vendors there, selling all sorts of interesting food. And he'd arranged to go with Tobias and Daniel. He was sure their mums wouldn't make them take food. Why was his mum always so fussy?

He saw his father shaking his head.

"Do as your mother says, son," he whispered. "It's only because she cares, you know."

"You can have some of the dried fish," she said, "and I've just finished baking some barley bread. It will be nice and soft to eat."

"Thanks, Mum," Zac mumbled. He watched as she parcelled up the five new loaves and the two salt fish. It seemed to take an age. He just wanted to get going.

"Now, you take care, and make sure you're back by nightfall," she said. She still looked worried.

"He'll be fine," said Dad. "Now, away, son."

At last he was on his way. The sun was quite high in the sky and it was already very hot. The road was dusty. And soon his feet were dirty grey. He would be ashamed if the preacher looked at him.

134

He had arranged to meet Tobias and Daniel at the edge of the town. There was no sign of them when he got there. They had probably set off hours ago for the hillside. They'd probably guessed that his mother wouldn't let him go and listen to the preacher. Well, they'd been wrong. But it had taken a long time to persuade her, and they'd probably given up waiting.

The crowds were already making their way up to hill just outside the town. Zac decided to follow them. He remembered how Daniel had told him all about the new teacher. His uncle had seen him a few months before.

"He made a blind man see!" shouted Daniel. "And he stopped Mad Mildred's seizure." He writhed around on the floor as if he were Mad Mildred. "He just put his hands on her head and shouted "Be gone, Lucifer!" and she stopped shaking."

"They even say he's brought a dead man back from the grave," Tobias added, in a whisper. "We've just got to go and see him."

Zac arrived at the sloping field. All the visitors were setting out their rugs on the ground. There were so many people. The sun was getting really hot now. Still there was no sign of Daniel and Tobias. Some stern-looking men were showing people where to sit. One of them looked at Zac and pointed to a rocky piece of ground. His heart sank. If he sat there, he'd be behind the tall man with the wide shoulders. He wouldn't be able to see a thing. The ground looked so hard, too.

"Not there!" said another of the men. "Remember, the Master likes the children to be near the front!"

Zac heard the tall man grunt.

"I don't know who they think they are," he said to the woman sitting next to him.

"They're the disciples," replied the woman. "They're going to help him become King of the Jews."

Zac's heart was pounding as he was shown to the front of the crowd. He would really be able to see the teacher closer to from here. Would he do anything really dramatic? Perhaps he would make a blind man see? Or make a lame woman walk again? And now he, Zac, son of a carpenter, was going to see another son of a carpenter close too. This carpenter was different, though. He was going to become the King of the Jews and he could perform magic.

Zac didn't have time to look for his friends. The crowd suddenly went quiet and some of the men he had seen earlier came and stood in front of them. There was someone else as well with them. He seemed to stand taller than the other men, but when Zac looked closely, he saw that he was in fact shorter and his shoulders were certainly narrower than those of the burly men around him. He looked almost as if he were gliding as he walked along, a little as if his feet weren't actually touching the ground.

That must be him. Zac's mouth went dry.

The preacher stepped forward from the other men. He looked carefully at the crowd. His eyes seemed to rest a few seconds on everyone. Zac gulped as two dark eyes looked into his. He was sure the man could understand every single thing in his head.

The teacher began to talk; he told them many stories of how they could all live together better. Zac could understand these stories, unlike the ones the priests had told him. Then came the magic. The preacher went around the crowd putting his hands on people. He helped one woman get up from a stretcher. She kissed the teacher's feet.

"Thank you Master," she said.

The preacher smiled gently at her.

He whispered something to a little girl who had not been able to talk and she was suddenly able to laugh and sing with her brothers and sisters. There were tears in her father's eyes as he thanked the preacher.

"Don't thank me," replied the preacher. "I am just going about my business."

He touched the eyes of a man who could not see. The man began walking a little unsteadily.

"So this is how beautiful the world is," he said. "This is what colour is."

"Now enjoy this creation," said the preacher.

Yes, this would certainly be something to tell his friends. But he wished he could hear more stories. He liked listening to the teacher's voice and all of what he had said seemed to make so much sense.

The preacher had stopped working now and was deep in discussion with his men. He was shaking his head. The disciples were shrugging their shoulders. It seemed as if there was an argument going on.

Zac suddenly realised how hungry he had become. He remembered the salt fish and the barley loaves his mother had given him. That would have to do. He had no money to buy anything from the vendors.

Vendors? Where were they? That was what was missing – the smell of freshly roast meat, the shouts of the wine merchants, bragging that their wine was the best and the baskets of bright colourful fruits. Of course! The Romans had forbidden them to attend when the teacher was talking or performing his magic. They didn't like this man people were saying was going to become King of the Jews.

One of the teacher's men walked up to where Zac was sitting.

"Does anyone have any food?" he asked. "Anything at all? We have to feed everyone. The Master doesn't want people to have to go into town."

Zac fiddled with his food parcel. That wouldn't go far

between – how many people were here? – He looked around him – five, six, maybe seven thousand. It was not as if it was anything very special either.

Then he remembered something the teacher had said – something about not worrying about what might happen, but just do whatever is right in any moment. It seemed right to offer his food.

"I've got five barley loaves and two salt fish," he whispered to the man. He thought for a moment that the man was going to laugh. He took the food from Zac, though.

"That'll be appetizing," someone behind him said.

"It'll sure go a long way amongst this lot," another voice said.

At that moment the teacher himself came over. He bent down and looked straight into Zac's eyes. Zac shivered, but it was a warm shiver as if sunlight had spread itself all through his body.

"Son," said the preacher. "You have done well. You have understood the will of Our Father."

He touched Zac's shoulder. The warmth spread through his body again, even stronger this time. He felt his cheeks go pink.

The teacher took the food from his disciple, and stood back. He held it in one hand and held the other hand over it. He looked up to the sky.

"Oh Lord Our Father," he said, "we thank You for providing the earth and sea, the sunshine and the rain, to produce this food, and the generosity in the heart of this young boy to share it with us."

Suddenly, from all parts of the crowd, people were shouting that they had food they wanted to give.

"I have a flagon of wine we can share!" shouted one.

"We have some lovely ripe grapes," cried another.

"I have seven unleavened loaves and a pound of figs," declared a third.

Soon everyone was giving something. A basket weaver had his cart nearby and he lent the preacher's men twelve baskets so that they could collect up the food and then take it round to the crowd. They went up and down the lines of people taking and offering food. The baskets seemed fuller each time they came around.

Zac had a wonderful supper. He did eat a little of the barley loaves and maybe a mouthful of the salt fish. But he also had fat black olives, softly crumbling goat's cheese and clear sweet honey on freshly baked bread. He was soon feeling full and actually turned down some food.

The preacher came over to him again.

"You have worked the magic this time, son," he said. "You showed the people what to do."

Zac's cheeks went even hotter than before. He felt himself grinning. The teacher grinned back. Suddenly, they were just two carpenters who understood the world, rather than King and worker.

The sun was completely down by the time Zac got home.

"Well," said his father, "what was the best bit? Did you see any magic?"

"Oh the best bit," said Zac, "was when the Master magicked up food for the crowd."

"Oh, what a waste of the bread and fish I sent with you," said his mother.

Zac smiled to himself. He couldn't wait to see Daniel and Tobias the next day.

Losing Tony

The clock on the church tower has just chimed two. She said she would be here at three. Lunch is over and done with at one. Even the dish washer is loaded. And now it has run. It's too early to unload it. Yet I can't settle to anything else. Will she be on time? I don't know. I don't know her at all. Is she like me? Does she waste a huge portion of her life being much too early for fear of being late? I don't even know whether I want her to arrive ahead of time, so that we can get it over with, or late so that I've got more time to get myself ready.

My stomach churns. Can I keep my lunch down? Will I be able to offer her tea and will we get round to eating the cake? Is it stupid to offer tea and cake on an occasion like this? At least the weather is warm. We can sit in the garden. Being outside always makes things seem better doesn't it?

She'll be a complete stranger, won't she? I've not met her before. Just that one time in a dream. When she was six or so and she'd managed to swim a length of the school swimming pool. I was standing holding a towel for her. Out of the water she came. Athletic and strong and at the same time so feminine and completely my little girl.

Now I can feel my own heart beating wildly and the hall clock ticking. They're in harmony. They are both counting my life away.

I think of the last time I saw Tony. It was a day just like this. We walked down to the corner shop to buy some ice cream. His idea and his treat. As usual I had to trot at his side like a pet dog. He eats well and he's a good cook. He remains thin because he walks everywhere and so fast. It's hard to keep up with him.

He's always been a bit of an enigma, my son, my first born. Yes he's tall and strong. Years of dancing, ice-skating as well as the fast walking have made him muscular and supple. He can be strong. He's got back up after blow upon blow. Yet he can cry buckets about a sad film or the death of an animal. He is so talented and creative – and messy. Out of chaos comes beauty.

He daydreamed as we ate the ice cream. It was as if he wanted to tell me something but couldn't quite get round to it. I knew, though, when he left that day we would never see him again. He confirmed this later by phone. And no, we've not seen him since. Not for over three months. We mourn him. He is gone from us. Forever.

I decide I must look my best to meet my unknown daughter. I'm glad I had my hair bleached white. It doesn't make me look old – quite the opposite. I'm sure Tony would have confirmed this and certainly his younger sister approves.

"Just, think, Mum, you could have purple streaks put in. Tony would have loved that," she says.

Yes I'm sure he would. Well at least I can go for purple eye shadow but I stick to a more conventional lipstick shade. Who knows what she'll be into?

I decide I can't slop around in my jeans. I must be smart even if I look casual. I select a top in the green that suits me so well, and my beige linen trousers. Will it do? If only I could ask Tony. He was always good at helping me to find the right clothes. I got that promotion when he chose the bright pink suit for the interview. That white linen skirt he found the day he got the job at Selfridge's lasted for years. And what about those high boots he picked out when we went on the day trip to France? I wish I could ask him now.

I look at the mugs and plates I've set out and decide

they're wrong. I open the china cabinet and get out our best tea set. This is an occasion. We must treasure it.

Seconds after the church clock chimes quarter to the hour I hear the clatter of heels on the footpath. I brace myself for the doorbell. I don't have to wait long. My mouth is dry as I make my way to the door. I see the silhouette of a very tall person through the frosted glass. It could almost be Tony. I am trembling so much that I can hardly open the door.

I manage at last and there she is. Soft blond curls frame her angular face. She is wearing a short shift dress in my green. What about that then. Size six, I would say. Size six for goodness sake. Well, at least she won't be stealing my clothes like Tony used to steal his father's. Her make-up is immaculate. Subtle. You can't really see it's there. A small patent leather bag hangs from her shoulder. Under her arm she is carrying what I recognise as a painting. It is wrapped in brown paper. She hands it to me. "This is for you. You might like to get it framed."

She slips off her jacket and sits down at the dining table as if she's been coming here for years.

I open the parcel. I recognise one of my book covers.

"Thank you," I say.

She nods and looks down at the table. "Oh you've got the best china out."

"Well it's a bit of an occasion, isn't it?"

She shrugs. "What's the cake?"

"Raisin parkin." I remember how much Tony used to like it.

She grins. Her face crinkles and her eyes are just like Tony's.

We chat. It's as if we've known each other for years.

Then though there is an awkward silence. She puts her

hand on my arm. "Should we go round to that picture-framers you told me about? I could help you chose something."

"That's a nice idea."

It's less than a mile away but it's too hot to walk. We take the car. We can't stop right outside. The primary school is emptying and lots of mums have come in cars. We have to park about four hundred yards away.

We set off.

She strides ahead. The heels don't faze her. I have to trot along, just like I did with Tony.

She pauses and turns. "Come on, Mum."

The sun catches her hair. She looks really pretty. My lovely daughter Toni.

Finding Story

"We're going to have to close the main gates now," said Tonga.

"But Bradley's not here yet," said Wimple.

"He'll have the sense to shelter," said Tonga. "He'll know what to do in the storm."

Wimple wasn't so sure. Bradley wasn't always the most practical person. But they'd been lucky, year on year. He'd always got through before the main gates were closed and he'd always got there in time to start the story-telling. There'd been storms before but never anything this bad.

"Just go and do it," said Tonga.

Wimple scurried off in the direction of the main gate.

"Tonga says we're to shut the gates down now," he said to Rupert.

The wind was really whistling now and the snow had more than half covered the entrance.

"Right-o," the guard answered. The gate clanged into place. Then there was a whirring sound. And then it was silent. The wind and the snow seemed to have stopped. All Wimple could hear now were the Yule songs and the sounds of people rushing backwards and forwards. Now as well there were glorious smells. Roast hog. Mint punch. Cherry pies. Somehow now that the noise had gone the food seemed even more enticing.

"I must say that's a relief," said Rupert. "I was so worried the water would come into the warren and we would all be drowned."

"But what about Bradley?" said Wimple.

"Bradley will be fine," said Rupert. "The moon-folk will offer him shelter."

Wimple hoped the guard was right. Yes, the moon-folk were generous enough if the stories about them were anything to go by. But would Bradley have the sense to seek one of them out?

A mouse in a footman's uniform scurried by, carrying a tray of roast chestnuts.

Wimple's mouth began to water.

Then the gong sounded.

Rupert rubbed his paws together. "Come on. Let's go and eat."

It was quite a good suggestion. The lobster soup was as delicious as usual. The hog had been cooked to perfection. The punch was sharp and warm at the same time. The pies were irresistible. Wimple managed six and only felt slightly sick afterwards.

Tonga sighed. "It's not the same without the stories though."

"No, indeed not." Rupert rubbed his eyes and looked as if he was going to cry.

Wimple really did feel sick now. What if something had happened to Bradley?

"Could we tell our own stories?" said Rupert.

Tonga frowned and scratched his forehead. "I don't see why not. Would they be interesting enough, though?"

Rupert shrugged. "We could give it a go, I suppose." He took his bugle and gave it three quick blasts.

All of the other small animals and elven folk stopped talking.

Rupert cleared his throat. "Ladies, gentlemen, elven folk, fellow burrow dwellers. Our story laureate has not yet arrived. We trust that the moon-folk will have sheltered him from the storm. But we think we should go ahead with the story-telling. So we invite each and every one of you to contribute one story. A success story. Or something funny that happened to you. Maybe a time when you were greatly surprised."

There was silence at first.

145

Then there were some whisperings.

"Rubbish, that, about the moon-folk," Wimple heard one of the young voles whisper. "There ain't no such thing. If Bradley's out in this storm, he's done for."

Wimple hoped the vole was wrong.

At last though, a tiny dormouse put up his hand.

Tonga nodded to him.

"Please sir," said the dormouse. "I can tell a story!"

"Get to it then, young man. Everybody listen up."

The dormouse told his story about the time a domestic cat hunted him. The cat had been frightened by a dog and dropped the dormouse but not before he had been taken two miles away from home. The dormouse had had quite a few adventures trying to find his way home. Then a young elf told about the time she had fallen into a rain puddle and had been helped out by a frog. A young frog volunteered the story of how a princess kept kissing him and then complained that nothing had happened. "She wanted me to turn into a prince, I think," said the frog.

Soon the stories were flowing one after the other. Wimple helped himself to several more mint punches. They made him relaxed and sleepy. He kept dozing off and somehow the stories got mixed up with his dreams.

Suddenly, though, he awoke with a start. There was a loud knocking at the main entrance to the burrow.

Rupert, who also appeared to have been snoring gently, suddenly jumped up and rushed off with his bunch of keys towards the main gate.

Wimple's little heart was beating fast as he listened in to the conversation going on at the gate. He'd recognise that voice anywhere. Bradley! And those other people must be moon-folk. He'd never seen them before. He hid behind one of the drapes so that he could look at them without them seeing him.

They were strange creatures. They were completely hairless and did not appear to wear any clothes. They moved very gracefully and they glowed like moonbeams.

"Come out from behind that curtain, Wimple. I can see you. Now, what can you offer a poor starving fellow to eat on this fine Yule Eve?"

Bradley sat himself down by the fire.

Wimple still couldn't move. He was so fascinated by the moon-folk. They floated round Bradley, moving silently.

"I didn't think they really existed," he said.

Bradley laughed. "Every story you hear is true, in its own way." He took a goblet of steaming mint punch that a young elf offered him. He took a sip and closed his eyes. "Ah. That's better."

A red squirrel bounded up with a plate containing roast hog sandwiches and two cherry pies. Bradley nodded his thanks.

Wimple watched as the moon-folk seemed to evaporate with the steam for the punch. They floated up the chimney and although the flames from the fire touched them they didn't get burnt.

"Where did they go?" he asked nobody in particular.

"Like all stories, they fade," said Bradley.

"Aren't they real?" asked Wimple.

"They're as real as all stories," said Bradley.

"Well, did they help you in the storm?" asked Tonga. "Didn't they give you shelter?"

Bradley shrugged. "The storm wasn't so bad really. The snow was soft, though, and it was difficult to see and to move quickly. The moonbeams showed me the way."

He'd called them moonbeams. Perhaps it was just the moon that lit his way. The moon-folk had all disappeared now. It was impossible to examine them any further. He would never know now. Had they ever actually been there?

147

"I suppose the young'uns will be too tired for Yule Eve stories now," said Bradley as he finished the rest of his second cherry pie.

"Oh, we've had some stories," said Tonga. He told Bradley how lots of people had offered their own stories.

"Splendid!" said Bradley. "Then I will tell you just one Yule Eve story and the rest will do for Yule Day. "Get everybody organised, Tonga."

Tonga rounded up all of those who not yet scurried of to their sleeping places. Wimple was amazed that so many of the youngsters were still awake.

"Ah yes," said Bradley as he looked at his young audience. "Young people are always the best at appreciating stories."

But not just the young people, thought Wimple, curling up his toes in excitement. What was Bradley going to tell them?

"My story tonight is from another world a little bit like our own but the animals don't talk there. It is a story about a very special baby. An angel – this is a messenger from the god that those people worship, a most beautiful creature with great silver and gold wings – had told the mother that she was going to give birth to that god's son." Bradley paused to take another sip of his mint punch.

Wimple's toes curled even further. This was going to be a good one.

148

About a Blue Car

It was oddly quiet at the Parkinsons' semi in East Oakham. Sal had just come back from the pub with fiancé, Matt, and was astonished that her mother and father were not back from the cricket match. It was getting dark now, despite it being the middle of June. They'd left the pub because the landlord had called last orders.

"I wonder where they are," said Sal.

"Oh, I wouldn't worry," said Matt. "Probably having coffee with someone or something stronger. Especially if they won."

He was probably right. After all, her dad was vice-president of the Crockley cricket club. Crockley was where he worked. They were playing East Oakham so this match had been considered rather significant.

"I'm not really worried." But she was tired and couldn't understand why. "And now that I've sat down I can't move."

"All right. I'll put the kettle on, shall I, and make a cup of tea?"

Sal nodded. She closed her eyes. She could hear Matt pottering about in the kitchen. The noise became fainter and then she woke with a start. Well, she hadn't really been asleep but she'd sort of had a dream. A bit vague really. Something about a dark blue car. She wasn't really sure what. But she could remember the number plate: MEM0 775 D. That wouldn't exist, would it?

"Here, drink this," said Matt as he placed a tray down on the table.

Sal took one of the mugs of tea and one of the digestive biscuits then picked up the TV remote.

She found a programme about mind-reading.

"You're even better than this guy," said Matt as she answered question after question correctly.

149

"It's just daft," said Sal. "I'm only guessing. I feel nice and relaxed, though."

"More tea?"

She nodded.

They'd just finished their second cup and the credits were beginning to roll when Sal heard the key in the lock.

"Sorry we're so late," said her mum. "Only we stopped to help this old lady who was run over."

"Oh dear," said Matt.

"Oh it was all right. The car was going very slowly. But she was a bit shocked and so was the driver of the car."

"We couldn't make him understand a word," said her dad. "I think he was foreign. Maybe the car was as well. Had a funny number plate. MEMO 775D."

Sal shivered.

"Which side was the steering wheel on?" asked Matt.

"Good point," said Mr Parkinson. "You know, I didn't notice."

"It was a blue car wasn't it?" said Sal. "And it was backing out of that alleyway next to the hairdresser – you know where them mucky kids used to play?"

"Yes," said Mrs Parkinson slowly.

"Bloody hell, what are you saying, Sal?" Matt's eyes were round and open.

"I saw it when I fell asleep when you were in the kitchen."

Nobody seemed to know what to say.

"You know, you're getting good at this clairvoyance malarkey," said Matt as they got ready for bed later. "Perhaps you should make a career of it."

"Mmm," said Sal. It hadn't been much use, though had it? It had been a bit of fun with the TV programme. And she hadn't really been worried about her mum and dad and even if she had been, having that vision or whatever it was hadn't really told her a lot. Still, it had seemed to happen because she was so relaxed and having Matt make her tea and feed her biscuits had been good. "As long as you keep on supplying the digestives and as long as you promise to make them chocolate."

Mobility

"I don't know," said Alfie. "We haven't renewed our driving license for years. Couldn't stand the fuss with all of the medicals."

He looked across at Jenny, waiting for her confirmation as usual. She nodded her head vigorously. It had been a joint decision after all. They managed very well these days with public transport and taxis.

"But the whole point is, you don't need a license to be allowed to operate the new transporter. Just your normal health check." Tompkins, the Transport Centre official, sucked in his cheeks and frowned slightly.

"That's it though. More health checks." Alfie looked at Jenny again. She was still nodding.

"You have to have them anyway, at your age." Tompkins' lips were tight as he spoke. "Didn't you enjoy the test drive?"

Alfie had to admit it had felt rather grand, gliding smoothly along in a smart new four-seater unit that hadn't been used by lots of other people. It had that new car smell he used to enjoy when he changed his four-by-four every three years. Back then he had a company car and would rather drive anywhere himself than be driven.

Tompkins had a point. Alfie scratched his head. "It's just such a lot of responsibility. What if something goes wrong?"

Tompkins sighed. "There have been so many safety checks. Even if it did crash it is so well constructed... an aeroplane could land on it and you'd still walk out alive. Its operation is so simple – voice controlled and already programmed to recognise both of your voices. Its intelligence will grow as it gets to know you. A toddler could operate one of these. And we picked you and your

152

good lady as you both so perfectly match our target customer."

Jenny nudged him. "It would be nice to be independent again, Alfie. And we could never afford one of these if we had to pay for it ourselves. Just think we could tootle up to London Dock and see the kids at the weekend." She had that look in her eyes. The one that said "Please Alfie. Go on. Just for me." Attached almost fifty years now and she could still get him to do anything.

Alfie sighed again. "All right then. Let's give it a go."

"It's really just that simple?" Alfie was sitting in what would be the driver's seat if the transporter had needed driving. Jenny was beside him.

"Sure is. You programme it yourself. Just tell it your address."

"Unit 7b, Cherry Orchards. Sector 6."

"Can you give me the full location code?" The transporter's voice startled him.

"It's Brad," whispered Jenny.

She was right. This seemed like a bit of a sick joke. They'd somehow managed to programme the transporter with the voice of their eldest son who had died suddenly three years ago from some as yet unidentified cause.

"Better give it the code," said the official. "And don't forget you can rearrange the seats. You don't really need to watch the road. You don't need to worry about travel sickness either. The motion of the vehicle has been customised."

"89436.43," mumbled Alfie.

The transporter glided smoothly out of the docking area and was soon making its way into the early evening traffic. Alfie wanted to steer, to put his foot on the brake to slow it down or push the accelerator to make it go faster. Yet even as he thought these things the transporter did exactly what he would have done in the traffic as it was now.

"Shall we turn and face each other?" Jenny touched his arm.

"I prefer to keep my eyes on the road," Alfie muttered.

His body seemed to anticipate every move that the transporter made. He realised after a while that it really was driving exactly the way he used to. He couldn't fault it. It made precisely the right move every time. There were no surprises.

He'd almost begun to relax – almost, not quite – when it turned into their little street and slowed down as it approached their house.

"Shall I go on to the drive or park in front of the house?" Alfie waited for the word Dad.

"Oh, in front of the house. We want the neighbours to see, don't we love?" She didn't seem perturbed by Brad's voice anymore.

"Your call." The vehicle lowered itself off the hover mode and sank to the ground. "Going to standby."

The doors opened and Alfie and Jenny stepped out. A neighbour was looking at them through one of the big picture windows at the front of their house. Jenny waved cheerily.

Over the next few days, Alfie spent a lot of time in the transporter, trying to find out what it could do. It was different from how he used to play with the controls when he'd got his new company car in the past; this one he quizzed it to find out what it could do. It was just as they'd said at the Transport Centre; it was entirely controlled by voice.

Jenny touched his arm gently when he came in for cup of coffee one day. "You do know it's not really Brad, don't you?"

"Of course." He shook her arm away. Of course he

knew it was only a damn machine. But it was rather good, talking to him man to man. Chatting about a car just like they would have done in the old days. The girls were all very well. He missed having another man in the family.

"We'll need to refuel him, soon."

"Him? I thought cars and things were always her?"

"Well this one's level-headed. It must be a he."

"Cheeky!" She hit the top of his arm playfully.

"I can go and refuel alone," Brad's voice came through the home dataserve.

Jenny's eyebrows shot to the top of her forehead.

Alfie shook his head. "I'd better go with him."

"It."

"There really is no need."

"Hang on. I'm coming."

"You really are an old fart sometimes, Dad," said the transporter's voice as Alfie settled himself into the mock driving-seat. "I'm perfectly capable of refuelling on my own."

"What about paying though?"

"You've forgotten that fuel is free for the first year? Honestly, Dad, you won't pass your medical next time and they'll take me away."

Amazing, that he'd called him Dad. Twice now.

The transporter jerked away from its parking spot. It wasn't the smooth ride they'd become used to this time. They'd gone on a few tootles, as Jenny had called it. To the shops, to the drop-in centre and just for a ride around town. "We've got to impress the neighbours," she'd said. And every time the transporter had behaved as if it was being driven by a perfect driver.

Not today though. It hurtled around. It stopped suddenly, almost throwing Alfie from his seat despite the strength of the force field belt. At one point it darted into a very small gap, causing the following vehicle to brake hard.

"Watch it," muttered Alfie.

"Don't you back-seat drive me. You have no right. You wouldn't be allowed near a normal car."

Brad was back. Alfie had forgotten he could be like that. It was usually when his blood-sugar had been too low because he'd not got his insulin dose quite right.

He stopped at one of the refuelling points on Broad Street. It was true. He didn't need Alfie with him. He just hooked up and the unit started charging him.

"That's better. I'm sorry I was so tetchy, Dad. But you know what I'm like when I'm low on fuel. Best remind me never to go below half empty."

The indicator on the recharge unit showed that Brad was now three-quarters refuelled.

"That is good. So good. Oh God, Oh God. Yes please." Brad's voice got hoarser and higher.

Perhaps that's why he'd wanted to be alone. A bit embarrassing having your old dad along with something like that going on. So in future he would send him on his own off to recharge.

Alfie left Brad alone for a few days after that. He couldn't face the lad. He knew he needed to reconfirm that really it was just a car and the voice was just a clever trick. He knew, though, that he was actually avoiding finding out the truth. He also wasn't sure which truth he wanted least – that there was something seriously spooky about this vehicle or that there wasn't.

"Fancy a tootle to the shops?" said Jenny.

Alfie shook his head.

Jenny touched him lightly on the shoulder. "We've got to see this through, haven't we? You do know that, don't you? We don't want to lose him. They'll take him away if we don't use him."

Alfie sighed. She was right. "I'll go and see if I can find out what else he does."

His heart thumped as he opened the door. The dashboard lit up straight away and a gentle whirring started.

"Dad, I'm sorry for being such a tart the other day."

"It's all right. I get it. I was young once as well." That didn't sound right. This was embarrassing. He should get *a* grip. This was only a fucking car.

"Well, maybe you can show me what else you can do. We've done the simple stuff. What about, say, going on a longer journey?"

"Sure. Only…"

"Well?"

"Dad, I'm sorry as well about, you know, about going off like that. It was my own fault, you see."

Alfie's mouth went dry. "Are you saying…?"

"Did I top myself? No, no. I just got careless."

"Careless?"

Silence.

"Brad?"

More silence.

"We'd like to know."

The whirring got louder. "Do you know, I've got a mystery tour function. You and Mum should try it. Just come out, ready for what sort of trip you'd like. I'll assess you and whisk you off somewhere special."

"Sounds like a plan."

"Only… er… if I need to recharge, best if I drop the pair of you off and let you get a drink…"

"Oh yeah, we can't have your mum listening to that, can we?"

"Sure can't. And I promise I won't get tetchy beforehand."

157

"You're on."

"Mystery trip then."

Jenny finished packing the basket. She'd already put in the picnic mat, the plastiglasses, the cutlery and the plates and dishes. Now she added a plastivase and some everlasting flowers.

"Do we really need that?" said Alfie. They'd always made the effort for the kids. Now it was just them. And Brad, of course.

"Perhaps he'll remember," she said.

Alfie nodded. He carried on filling the cool box. Sandwiches – cheese and pickle, salmon and cucumber, ham and tomato. Salad. Carrot cake. Shortbread. White wine for Jenny and one small beer for him. And water for both of them.

Jenny touched his arm.

"You could put in a couple more, you know. You don't have to drive, remember."

Alfie nodded. He put in the extra bottles but he told himself he probably wouldn't drink them. He wanted his wits about him today.

They made their way out to the car.

"Well, this is exciting," said Jenny, as she fastened her seat belt.

Alfie didn't feel excited though. He just dreaded what Brad had in store for them.

The dashboard lit up. The whirring started.

"Your request?" Brad's voice was distant today.

"That mystery trip you promised."

"Very well." The vehicle was now completely ready to go. "You've got the measure of us then?"

Alfie looked at Jenny.

She shrugged "Look well if he takes us to a smart city."

158

"No. I can see you're ready for a picnic. The weather is fine in certain parts of the island. I'll get you to one of them in time for lunch."

Alfie took Jenny's hand and squeezed it. She squeezed his back.

Brad set off down the road, out of the estate and towards the edge of town. Soon they were speeding towards the suburbs, then through them and out into the countryside. Some of the factory farms still had big brown and white cows feeding on real grass.

"It's a shame it's just for show, isn't it?" said Jenny.

"It isn't," Brad suddenly snapped. "It was a genuine experiment in getting back to basics."

Alfie looked at the fuel reading. "How about stopping at a rest area? We'll grab a coffee while you recharge."

"Already?" Jenny raised an eyebrow.

"Yeah. Why not. We've got all of the time in the world."

The rest area was crowded though not overfull. There was a buzz about the place.

"That was always part of the fun, wasn't it?" Jenny stared at her cup of steaming coffee. The she looked around. "You know, it hasn't changed all that much really, has it?"

He had to agree. It hadn't. The same sort of people came there, apparently. The coffee was as good as ever. Only the way of paying was different. They used iris-scanners instead of plastic.

"20% seniors' reduction," said the electronic voice.

"I wish they wouldn't," hissed Jenny. "Giving our age away like that."

They were soon on their way again. The farms gave way to craggy ground. Up and up they went. They could see snow on the more distant mountains. The roads became less busy.

"I suppose it might have been frantic on the tunnel road," Jenny whispered.

They didn't discuss where they were going. They knew. They also knew he might be bringing them this way because this was the way they used to come before the tunnels were built.

Brad remained silent.

At last they started descending. They could see the blue sea in the distance. It still thrilled Alfie to come down from the mountains and see the sun catching the top of the waves. It was a glorious day, just right for a picnic.

Brad made his way through the old town, back out the other side, through the little seaside village where they used to sometimes hire a cottage, whose back garden was right on the beach, and then out along the bumpy road that lead to the dunes. They didn't feel the bumps, of course, because he hovered above them though he did gently follow their contours.

He parked on the hard sand. "I could of course take you down to the sea shore but it will be more like the old days if I stay here and you go along the boardwalk."

Alfie and Jenny both nodded.

It was indeed like old times. They felt the soft sand between their toes. Later it mixed with their sandwiches. And after a decent interval, and when their lunch had gone down, they bathed in the almost warm sea.

"Remember how they used to make slides on the dunes?"

"And how they used to bury each other?

"And how we played piggy in the middle and Katie always cried because she never could catch the Frisbee."

"Unless Brad helped her."

"Then they grew out of it."

"We never came again, did we, after Sandra got her first boyfriend?"

And it wasn't actually the same, anyway. You weren't allowed to make slides in the dunes anymore because that sort of activity ruins them. There were no children around, either. Not just because it was term-time and they'd be at school. No, seaside holidays like that weren't cool for kids any more.

Alfie, of course, had, despite his good intention, drunk more beer than he would if he'd had to drive the car and was feeling a little sleepy and more than a tiny bit bloated.

When they got back to the car there was the small matter of sand between their toes. They didn't want to make a mess of the inside of the vehicle that didn't really belong to them.

"Better do my ma's old trick." Jenny took one of Alfie's socks and started beating the sand off his foot. "Now don't put your foot back down until you've got your shoe and sock on."

She repeated the performance on the other foot and then used the tea-towel on her own feet. A little later they were ready to go.

"Well," said Brad. "How was it?"

"Good. It brought back some memories."

"I can hear a 'but' Dad."

"Well." He'd forgotten that sand could actually be unpleasant. It was a shame there hadn't been any kiddies. And he missed actually staying sober so that he could take care of everyone.

"I know Dad. It's not quite the same is it?"

"No, better get home, I suppose."

"Right. We'll go the quick way, through the tunnels. But we'll make one more stop on the way."

The Beach View hotel was busy enough to be cheerful but not so busy that it felt crowded. The view was glorious. A calm sea tipped small-lipped waves on to flat toffee-coloured sands. Through the picture windows they could see sea-birds flying across the sky. The air in the hotel, Brad informed them, had an ozone-like substance added that made it feel like outdoor sea air but without any disturbing change in temperature. Alfie and Jenny sipped their cocktail. Sea-breath, Brad had recommended. It was good. Far from making Alfie feel more bloated and intoxicated it seemed to be waking him up, giving him more energy, making his thoughts clearer.

"You see, the new is good also." They'd done as Brad had asked and transferred the car's memory to their portables." Isn't it nicer having the nature-carpet underneath your feet rather than crude sand? And can't you see the sense of the bio-aware drinks? As you touch the sensor it takes a body reading and adjusts the drink to suit your current stage of metabolism."

"But I thought you liked the old ways?" Jenny was almost choking on her drink.

"I do. But they should only be used for nostalgic purposes. That was my mistake."

"Mistake?" What was Brad trying to tell them? Alfie's mouth was dry now and his heart was beating faster than normal. It was going to take one heck of a bio-aware drink to sort this one out.

"I tried to control the diabetes by diet alone. I gave up on the science."

"But why couldn't they tell that?" Surely with all the science they could use these days they should have been

162

able to figure it out? Didn't this just prove that scientists didn't know everything?

"I was so far off the scale, Dad. You'd better order another drink. Then once you're settled we'd better head back."

"So what has the performance been like?" Tompkins was taking it in turns to stare into Brad's interior and at the tablet he was holding.

Alfie couldn't guess what all of those figures meant that were skittering across the tablet's screen. "Doesn't that thing tell you?"

"Oh, yes, we've all the technical data here." Tompkins frowned slightly.

"Is there a problem?" Alfie dreaded that they might want to recall the vehicle, that they might want to take Brad away from them for a second time.

"No, not really." Tompkins scratched his head then shook it. "It's just that the intelligence centre seems to have used up a great deal of memory."

"Does that matter?"

Tompkins shrugged. "It doesn't seem to. Everything else seems to be functioning well." He turned and looked Alfie straight in the eyes. "What I really want to know is, how has it been for you?"

"He's been very good. Excellent. We couldn't do without him." Jenny blushed as Tompkins looked at her surprised. He clearly thought that women of Jenny's generation had no interest in technical matters.

"Good, good," muttered Tompkins as he tapped something into his tablet.

"Er, will we be allowed to keep him?" Alfie dreaded his answer.

Tompkins grinned. "I love the way you both call the vehicle him. Does he have a name?"

163

"Brad," said Alfie and Jenny together.

"Sweet! Yes, of course you can keep him. But from now on you'll have to pay for recharges yourselves and once it wears out we can't replace it for you."

Alfie nodded. Jenny squeezed his hand. He squeezed hers back.

"So clever. How you got our son's voice on there. And how you got the intelligence to work just like Brad would. Isn't it Alfie?"

"Really?" Tompkins typed something into his tablet. "Thought so," he said. "Standard male navigator. He scratched his head again. "That might explain why it took up so much memory." He turned and grinned at them. "Amazing, uh?"

Other Publications by Bridge House Imprints

Links

by Dianne Stadhams

LINKS – sometimes random, many times unplanned, often with far reaching consequences, always shaping our journey from cradle to grave – the stuff of life.

Just how do Atta Gatta the child-eating crocodile, Scheherazade the pantomime star and Judy the stammering Goth strategically connect characters across the globe?

Enjoy this trilogy of inter-linked short stories that will make you smile and squirm as they raise questions about the needs and challenges of our contemporary world.

Order from Amazon:

Paperback: ISBN 978-1-907335-63-1
eBook: ISBN 978-1-907335-64-8

The Art of Losing

by Paul Williams

In this internationally-acclaimed collection of contemporary literary fiction stories by Paul Williams we are invited to appreciate what it means to master the art of losing – to let go of things both big and small – whether it be dreams, or love, or houses, or whole continents. Told with wit, humour and pathos, the stories reveal the unexpected narratives that often flow beneath the surface of contemporary lives.

The twenty stories lurch from continent to continent across Australia, Europe and South Africa, from child to teen to adult, from past to present, from war to peace, from me to you.

Order from Amazon:

Paperback: ISBN 978-1-907335-61-7
eBook: ISBN 978-1-907335-52-5

Keepsake

by Jenny Palmer

Keepsake and Other Stories is an anthology of short stories
by one of the growing number of brave women writers.
Jenny Palmer brings us stories of otherness, witchcraft and
magic close to home and further afield within Europe. We
meet all sorts of characters: those who rely on guard dogs,
those who shun social media and those who are obsessed.
We even meet a Neanderthal man. There are paranormal
stories, a story of bad neighbours, and a story of
redundancy. And many more. All to be enjoyed.

"Jenny is totally in control of her stories. They are memorable
and perfectly crafted." (*Amazon*)

Order from Amazon:

Paperback: ISBN 978-1-907335-57-0
eBook: ISBN 978-1-907335-58-7

140 x 140

by Gill James

This anthology of women's fiction, this collection of very
short stories, some might say a flash collection, is thought-
provoking and each story is based upon a tweet. Except that
each piece is 140 words long and not 140 characters.

"Inspiration for stories can come from a vast array of
sources but, in this entertaining book from Gill James, she
chose the first picture she saw on her Twitter feed on
specific dates. Those dates form part of the stories and, as
the title suggests, there are 140 of them, each of 140 words.
This is a fantastic achievement. Some tales are laugh out
loud funny, others are thoughtful, some you root for the
characters, and there are tragic stories too. Whatever your
mood, you will find plenty to suit you here." *(Amazon)*

Order from Amazon:
ISBN: 978-1-910542-35-4 (paperback)
978-1-910542-36-1 (ebook)

Chapeltown Books

Clara's Story: a Holocaust Biography

by Gill James

Clara will not be daunted. Her life will not end when her beloved husband dies too young. She will become a second mother to the young children who live away from home at a rather special school – a particular class of disabled children growing up in Nazi Germany.

Clara's Story: a Holocaust Biography is the second story in the Schellberg Cycle. It might be described as a tragedy or it might be described as a story of survival. In the end it is up to the reader or even Clara herself to decide.

"The social history starting before World War 1 and continuing to the present day, was extremely interesting and Clara herself had the attitude that where there's hope there's life. A well-written and thought-provoking book." *(Amazon)*

Order from Amazon:
ISBN: 978-1-910542-33-0 (paperback)
978-1-910542-34-7 (ebook)

Chapeltown Books

January Stones

by Gill James

These stories were written one a day throughout January 2013. They were originally published on a blog called Gill's January Stones. Sometimes the stories would come right at the beginning of the day. Sometimes they would take a while longer.

Do they have a theme? Not really, though the idea of 'stones' is one of turning them over slowly on the beach until we find the right one.

There was no strict word count. Each story is as long as it needs to be. It had to be finished, though, by midnight of that day.

"The book is a quirky, easy read and most entertaining. Some of the stories make your blood run cold, others amuse, others are interesting character studies. If you want something a little bit different, this is a great place to start."
(Amazon)

Order from Amazon:
ISBN: 978-1-910542-10-1 (paperback)
978-1-910542-11-8 (ebook)

Chapeltown Books

www.ingramcontent.com/pod-product-compliance
Lightning Source LLC
Chambersburg PA
CBHW072356190626
46811CB00019B/900